put them all together,
they spelled horror

A beautiful young widow who demanded sexual gratification each time she allowed one of her late husband's files to be opened.

A millionaire haunted by a secret buried deep in the past—a secret brought to life by a mocking voice on a tape recorder.

A brilliant lawyer with a great ponderous body, spindly legs, a capacity for infinite deception, and a mysterious set of sinister instructions.

And entangled with them all, a man named Kenneth Leeds, trapped in a nightmare of another man's dreaming, a puppet in the hands of a corpse . . .

the dinosaur

lawrence kamarck

A SIGNET BOOK from
NEW AMERICAN LIBRARY
TIMES MIRROR

Library of Congress Catalog Card Number: 68-14533

This is an authorized reprint of a hardcover edition published by Random House, Inc. The hardcover edition was published simultaneously in Canada by Random House of Canada Limited, Toronto.

SIGNET TRADEMARK REG. U.S. PAT. OFF. AND FOREIGN COUNTRIES
REGISTERED TRADEMARK—MARCA REGISTRADA
HECHO EN CHICAGO, U.S.A.

SIGNET, SIGNET CLASSICS, MENTOR AND PLUME BOOKS
are published by The New American Library, Inc.,
1301 Avenue of the Americas, New York, New York 10019

FIRST PRINTING, JUNE, 1970

PRINTED IN THE UNITED STATES OF AMERICA

to caroline

It is indeed most fortunate for us, as well as for all living creatures, that dinosaurs vanished from the earth. Even the smaller species would have proved a terrible menace to human beings, and one's imagination is staggered at the thought of the carnage a single, living Tyrannosaurus would inflict upon a community.

—*Strange Prehistoric Animals and Their Stories*
by A. Hyatt Verrill

One

IT'S A STRANGE BUT VERY REAL AND HORRIFYING DREAM. I have it quite often. After you dream one thing over and over again, you begin to think that it's true. If it is, I murdered a lovely woman.

She wasn't lovely in the dream. Elizabeth was standing by a door, screaming at me. "Get out!" she shouted. "I don't want you here!" She leaped at me and pushed. Her fingers clawed at my arms. There was a ringing sound, incessantly punctuating every move we made. Suddenly she ran away from me down a hallway bright with light.

I followed. She turned and backed away from me. She looked frightened. Step by step we moved as in a dance. She was standing finally in a kitchen. She said, "Oh, my God, I knew it would be now." And she whirled about. She had her head raised so that her throat was exposed.

There was a large piece of glass by the sink. I took it up and drew it with a quick slash across her throat. I let her fall. I went back to the door, opened it and left. On the other side stood a Tyrannosaurus, its enormous jaws slack. It seemed to be smiling. I closed my eyes, and on opening them, found the monster gone. All that was left was its black shadow.

I would then wake up.

This is the story of a murder that another man planned, still another did, and one that I dream about. It is a murder that I might have done.

It's also the story of a man named Morgan Harper Stimmes.

Two

I THINK OF MORGAN HARPER STIMMES DURING THE HOLIDAY season when I hear the tinkle of glasses. I don't believe that I would be very startled if I were to look up at the next party I attend and see the towering blond-haired Stimmes weaving his way through the crowd, laying a hand on a shoulder of a stranger and ducking to whisper some inanity, which even a stranger might enjoy, slipping by (satisfied and smug to have caused a smile) to a pretty woman to plant a kiss on her cheek and a compliment in her ear and finally to come to me and greet me, as always, "Leeds, I suspect—just suspect, mind you—that everything is better than it was when it was just wonderful." Then he'd tip his head back and howl with delight at his own fine optimism.

My name is, of course, Leeds—Kenneth Leeds—and I was Morgan Stimmes' best friend, even though I was ten years younger and had almost nothing in common with him. The basic difference between us rested, in great probability, in that he gained his maturity during that bauble of a time, the twenties, and I opened my eyes as a young man in that gray time, the thirties.

I have described myself as Morgan's best friend, though in truth I would have described myself as more of a casual one, but Morgan often said I was his best. And perhaps I was, for he chose me to straighten out his untidy affairs after he died. There is some irony in that statement, and perhaps it's bitter.

Morgan telephoned me. His voice, ordinarily the triumphant peal of a deep-sounding Sunday chime, was a coarse whisper of itself. I was surprised that it was Morgan, for I had never known him to be sick.

"Damn it, Leeds," he said, "I want to know if you can come down to New York and visit with me. It'll have to be tomorrow, because I might lose all speech before too long."

"The day you lose all speech, you'll be dead," I joked.

"That's precisely why I called you. I'm about to die."

I hesitated for a moment. I thought he was joking. He had always talked of death as unlikely, illogical, and unnecessary.

"I realize that I have purposefully used a distasteful and unforgivable, even shocking, appeal, but the truth remains the truth. I will be dead sometime within the next month," he continued in rasping atonality.

"You're not joking," I said, experiencing for an instant the loss I'd feel if Morgan Stimmes were indeed to die.

"It's just possible that the gods are finding my situation something of a joke, but it's their joke, not mine. Now, please tell me if I can see you tomorrow."

I deliberated for a quick second, not because I was considering such practical matters as arranging for a substitute to take over my classes for the next day, but because I was not thoroughly convinced that Morgan was serious.

"I need to see you." And he ended this plea with a wheezing cough.

"Of course I'll come," I said. There could be no doubt now. Morgan, for as long as I had known him, had never needed. For him to say that he needed was a shock all by itself, almost as powerful as the thought that he was dying. Perhaps, in some ways, more.

My first meeting with him, when I was Assistant to the Publisher of *Signal Magazine,* has vividly stayed in my mind.

I had a small windowless and almost airless office, perhaps bigger than a coat closet. My position resembled that of an army orderly. I had to keep the publisher's office in liquor and run errands. I also was able to be officiously important in dealing with mere magazine laborers, writers, and editors.

At the moment the publisher was interested in replacing the managing editor, whom he had discovered having lunch with the owner of a competitive journal. I was assigned the task of speaking with likely replacements in order to weed out the usual number of editorial charlatans who inhabit that strange world and have accumulated impressive titles and credits by dint of luck and bravado. *Signal* had had one of these, and he had loaded the staff with drinking cronies and incompetents.

When Morgan first entered my office, I was certain that he was one of the successful frauds. It was not only his appearance. There was a devil-may-care look about the way he dressed. He was wearing a brown and baggy tweed suit with suede patches on the elbows, a blue button-down shirt open at the collar, no tie. Usually this sort of costuming is calculated for its effect: the dashing-man-about-town.

I was troubled by the very fact that he had been willing to apply for a job by seeing me first. He was one of the more noted war correspondents, being one of the very few who could write of the war in terms of his own personal adventures. (He produced two successful books, and the most popular of the two bore the title *My War*.) I believed that Stimmes' reputation must have been over-blown just because he was in my office and had not insisted on going directly to the publisher.

With one big hand he held onto the door frame and leaned into my office. His deep tan, by contrast, made his yellow hair appear to be almost white. I was surprised at his youthfulness. He looked to be a boy entering his twenties. I knew it was not possible for him to be that young, if only because of the stories about him told in the bars and editorial offices of New York. There was the fabulous one of his prodigious drinking bout at the Shepheard's Hotel in Cairo three years before. As Rommel's troops chased across the desert closer and closer, Stimmes and five other journalists agreed that it would be a terrible shame to have the hotel's fine supply of brandies and champagne fall into German hands.

According to the story, Stimmes was the only one of the six who was still conscious when the last case of champagne was brought from the cellar. "It occurs to me," he supposedly said as he staggered to his feet, his eyes pinned to the case, "that I better lend Monty a hand in slowing down Rommel. That last case will take me a little time." He swayed out of the hotel and then disappeared for two days. The next time he was seen was near El Alamein, leading in one hundred Italian soldiers who had surrendered to him. "Stay away from Old Man o'

War," went out messages from editorial offices. Stimmes had talked his five drinking companions into putting the cost of their bout down on their expense accounts.

A true story? I don't know. Many thought it was true, and it could have been. It wasn't until the war was well over that reporters bragged about being sick in LST landings. But times change.

Before standing to greet Stimmes, I glanced down at his résumé on my desk in order to check his age. He was not, of course, a youth, and he was also not an ancient. He was forty.

"I don't understand what I'm doing here," he said. His gray eyes wandered coldly about the closeness of the room, from my green file cabinets, which filled one wall, to the straight-backed guest chair, to the wall containing my Rand McNally map, on which I played at distant war with colored bulb-topped pins. He stared disdainfully at my map. Then he studied me, finally noticing that I stood unevenly. (My childhood struggle with infantile paralysis had left me with one leg shorter than the other.) His eyes softened. I felt his understanding and was grateful that it was not touched with pity.

"Mr. Stimmes?" I held out my hand.

"I'm sorry for my outburst a moment ago. I hadn't expected to be channeled. I rarely find it advantageous to talk to assistants of any kind. I don't mean that as a slight to you. It's just that I find such sessions infuriating, and I'm afraid I become insulting. I much prefer good manners, don't you?"

I don't know why, but I laughed. And then he laughed.

"Hell, Leeds . . . that's your name, isn't it?"

"Ken Leeds."

"I'll call you Leeds, if that's all right, and you can call me any damn thing you please. Let's go out and have a drink. I think we can get on famously if we could only get out of this black little hole." He swept a hand in a wide gesture to indicate his meaning.

It was not my habit to drink during the day, but I could not resist the invitation. I was convinced he was an acceptable candidate for the job of managing editor and I had only to learn if he was indeed the incredible drinker he was reputed to be. I realized that I could not, with honesty, say that I had interviewed Stimmes, and admitted to myself that my first impression of him totally swayed me. My real motivation rested entirely on my desire to spend an idle hour with a man who had experienced more of the war than anyone I had known.

We went to Kup's, a spacious place only by comparison with other bars. There were only a few others drinking, a few eating, uncomfortably perching over their tables on high dark-wood benches. The walls were covered with photographs of uniformed men, grinning with doleful gaiety.

Sitting high on tall stools, we drank and smoked in a fitful way, as most strangers do when first meeting, and we slowly began to talk, straying far from the subject that supposedly brought us to Kup's.

As we hopped from topic to topic, Stimmes' eyes glowed, sparkled with the excitement of a person who was finding everything said, my phrases as well as his own, as new as if we were the first people to speak on this planet. He created a magic with his enthusiasm. There was importance for me to be in his presence; he made me feel that I could not have devised a better way to spend the afternoon. Although I'm well aware that nothing I said had brilliance, I felt wise and good. There was one thing he said that I still am shaken by, and it wasn't far removed from simple barroom philosophy. I instantly understood its tragic implications for me as well as for Stimmes.

"We're presented with a bottle, a wine of life, if you would permit me a lousy metaphor," he said. "Inside is everything a man can experience. I don't know who's right, but some of us take the bottle and try to gurgle it all down so that every drop is taken. Perhaps it's fear of missing out—that life will not be long enough to finish it. Perhaps it's optimism—that when one bottle is empty another will come to replace it."

"What about the rest of us?" I asked.

"The ones who drink slowly? I'd say that they have somewhat the same alternatives. They drink slowly because they're optimistic that they'll live long enough to finish it. They fear that there is only one bottle, and if they finish it too rapidly, life is over."

I realized then that we had chosen differently. Was "choice" the word? I don't remember having decided that I would drink my wine slowly. I knew it was my way of life, the sipping. I wasn't certain that I was either afraid or optimistic.

"I can't fit myself into your metaphor," I said.

"And neither can I find a fit," he said. "I used to offer two other reasons for the two appetites, gluttony and moderation." He pursed his lips for a moment in thought. His eyes turned upward as if following a curl of cigarette smoke. He grinned suddenly, and our eyes met. "Hell!" he said. "I'm no glutton. I'm positive there's another bottle of wine in the closet, and I know I can't have it until I'm done with the first. I mean—really done!"

It has always struck me as strange that Stimmes did not become the magazine's managing editor. I know he was under consideration by the publisher: Stimmes was one of five men whose files rested in the middle of his desk. Three of those served varying terms as managing editor during the next year and a half. The fourth worked out perfectly. So the result of my interview of Stimmes was only that he and I became friends.

Walking through Grand Central station the morning after I had talked to Stimmes on the telephone, I realized that I had not been to New York for almost a year. I paused while crossing the lower-level waiting room. As I looked about, I wondered why I was never shocked by the steady creep of shoddiness in the station. There was an exhibit poured across one side of the floor, a sort of neon wash, proclaiming the suburbanite's need for power tools. In its stands stood glossy glassy middle-aged men next to flashy steel-blue machinery. Once Stimmes and I dashed across that cave in order to catch a train to Rye. We missed it. He turned to look at the station he had just run through. He stared at the jittery blue phosphorescent displays and shops unbelievingly. "I must have been away," he said as though to himself. "When did it happen?" he asked me.

"If you mean the . . ."

"The ugliness," he interrupted. I smiled. "Doesn't it bother you?" he asked.

"Bother me? I suppose I accept it for what it is—present-day America." It was an inadequate answer, but I wasn't prepared to analyze our boom culture; I was still exhausted from my limping run.

"The damned war," he said bitterly, "changed everything for the worse."

I finally left the station, thinking somberly that the war had indeed changed everything. Everything and everyone I knew, except Stimmes, had changed. The strange puzzlement I had seen in his gray eyes that day in Grand Central station had seemingly increased each time I saw him since. I've seen children who have had that look just after their parents move to a new neighborhood. But their eyes heal with time and adjustment. Stimmes' never did.

I went ouside and hailed a taxi and gave the driver Stimmes' address.

I had never been to Morgan's during daylight. This morning I was viewing the outside of the apartment for the first time unhampered by night. It was a sad time of the year, late autumn. This morning was cloudy. The buildings around Washington Square seemed desolate—even that row of brownstones on the north side, which normally have a scrubbed chintzy lived-in look. Morgan didn't live in one of those.

When he had first come to the city, he had rented a set of rooms across the Square in what was apparently a fine old building. It had once boasted of tenants who were bankers, publishers, lawyers. His rooms were palatial by today's standards of New York apartments. There were three bedrooms, a living room, a dining room, a kitchen. The ceilings were high and the windows were airily wide, framing a view of the park. In 1927, when Morgan returned from Paris, apartments of this sort were not simply rented because someone could afford them; they were passed on within a family. In this case, a cousin had died, and Stimmes' father was trustee of the cousin's estate.

I glanced up to the top window and thought I saw someone by the curtains looking down at me. I was about to wave but decided not to, because I couldn't believe that Morgan was watching for me, waiting. I had never known him to anticipate, either a person or an event. It passed through my mind that if he were really dying, I might find that many things had changed my friend.

There was an old elevator in the building, but I decided I would rather walk the stairs than use it. During evenings, in the expectation of going to a Stimmes party, it might have been possible to trust that rattling conveyance, but in broad daylight no, never.

I heard a door open upstairs and a shuffling of feet. "Morgan!" I called. Then I hurried as fast as I was able. And finally I reached the turn in the landing near the top and saw him. I was shocked to see how pale he had become. His body was bent, as if that mountain of a man had caved in. He stood there breathing deeply, as though he had been the one who had climbed five flights of stairs.

As I approached, bounding the last few steps, he offered his hand. We were like brothers for a moment; we were greeting one another as though for the last time.

"I'd like to talk a minute before we go in," he said. His voice was a whisper, a formulation of breath.

I nodded.

He glanced at his apartment door, as though someone might be there. "Here," he said, gesturing toward the top stair. "We'll sit here for a while."

We both settled down to the step. I thought then that this was only because of exhaustion. Remembering his phone call, I assumed that every move he made tore one small piece of his life from him.

"Did you notice someone at the curtain when you arrived?" he asked.

"I thought I did," I said. I wondered why he asked.

"I wanted to write you," he said, "but I no longer had the time. I've remarried—six months ago. Her name is Elizabeth. There's no time to explain. Remember, you know about her. I've written about her. Please do this for me, please."

It was difficult for me to understand everything he said, but those words I understood linked the others into meaning. I felt the terrible urgency of following his directives, to answer his plea. He didn't have to explain to me.

"Of course," I said.

He smiled, a smile smaller and less extravagant than in the old days.

When we rose, I attempted to help him up, but he brushed aside my offering hand. I thought to myself that he was an invalid who had not yet and might never accept his condition.

And so we entered his apartment. He put his arm around my shoulder. He leaned none of his weight on me. I realized then that though the gesture was natural for friends, it was meant as part of a display, a show for an audience. Elizabeth was about to meet an old friend. I wondered what else my part entailed.

Again daylight played its shabby trick with my sense of nighttime illusion. This apartment during the evening parties, the dinners, was magnificent. The first touch of change that light made was the mirror, an exquisite Mexican carved piece. I noticed that its sharp edges were nicked and dulled. The mirror itself seemed unreflective, dim—a collection of lustrous dust. And then in the doorway I saw her. My disillusion with the corrosion of the daylight world on the hard items in Morgan Stimmes' life vanished. Here was Elizabeth.

Had I seen her in one of Gauguin's gaudy Edens, I would have initially thought that she didn't belong. But she did. There was something in her face that gave me the feeling of primitive force, a sense of being in the presence of it.

She was so very slight, I thought at first that she was not fully adult, a sort of miniature human. I believe that if my expectation had not been that I would meet Stimmes' wife, I might have assumed that I was meeting a young woman of perhaps sixteen. This was no child.

"Elizabeth," I said.

"Mr. Leeds. I was so certain that I was right when I was watching from the window."

I dropped my eyes to my leg, painfully self-conscious of my limp for a moment.

"I told Morgan that I had seen a man handsome beyond description," she continued, "but he said I was wrong, for you were simply beyond description. I was right."

A faint blush had colored her cheeks. Without doubt she had made a comment to her husband about my limp. I had been with a limp for most of my life, and it had finally ceased to embarrass me. But on this greeting, I was aware of it, for I felt it marred me. I wanted Stimmes' wife to like me and admire me. Her flowery little speech was not honey, as perhaps she intended; it was salt.

"Ever since I met you," Morgan said in my ear, "I've been describing you to Elizabeth in letters." (I looked at Elizabeth anew, astonished at the information that Stimmes had known her longer than he had known me.) Then Morgan, his slate voice trailing with him, a rasping scratch, crossed the living room. He had not the volume to reach me, and so, reluctantly, hesitant to leave the immediate company of Elizabeth, I followed.

"Coffee?" Elizabeth's tinkling question abruptly stopped me. I turned to her again. This woman was indeed a difference in this home. I had known two of Stimmes' wives before her. The first—a tall black-haired beauty with enormous hips—always asked Stimmes' guests what kind of "hootch" they wanted and whether they wanted it diluted. The second never asked. Within seconds after arrival in the Stimmes household, the guest was handed an exotic concoction she had found the recipe for in a bartender's manual. This wife had what Morgan called a "sexual nature." A skinny silky handsome blonde, she converted the manual's titles to ones of her own liking. A Ward Eight was, of course, on delivery from her hands, "an Anatomical Kiss." A Ward Eight is no delight even with its own name; it was sickening with hers.

Perhaps I'm not being entirely fair to the two former wives; I had never been entertained by them during the morning. However, a young man who once served as Stimmes' secretary told me that he had never been offered anything less potent than beer in that household.

I was so pleased that Morgan had finally found a wife who regarded coffee as a suitable beverage that I said yes immediately. And I looked at Morgan. He was ponderously nodding his head. Had the lion been tamed? I wondered.

Then she was gone, leaving behind only a fragrance.

I crossed the room to Morgan. "Where did you find her?" I asked.

"Do you like her?"

"Very much."

"She's yours to beware of after I'm dead." He was staring after her, his eyes as emotional as buttons. A macabre insensitive comment? I was only conscious of its sense of finality. I wondered why his manner seemed so detached for such a thing as dying. Was this then what a man like Morgan does with the knowledge of his own death? Does he reduce the final episodes of his life to routine assignments? I have seen secretaries deal with the last days of their office, shuttle among their papers with tear-stained cheeks and glazed frightened eyes.

His gray eyes moved to me. "Do you have any doubts that I'll be dead soon?"

There were no doubts. His voice already sounded dead. In the grayness of his complexion I could see the blackness that would soon come. I attempted to speak, feeling that I should protest, for hope, I believe, was the gift to humanity from God, not speech or mind or thumbs or any of the multitude of trifles man is grateful for.

He shook his head quickly. "Please accept it as a fact. She won't. She can't, but I know you can. If I don't die, and that's an impossibility, you and I will have a bottle of champagne. Would it help if I added a redundancy to 'impossibility' and say a complete impossibility?"

He and I both smiled over this gruesome joke.

"Good," he said. "I didn't call you about Elizabeth. There's something else you can do for me."

"Anything," I said.

He studied me, suddenly. I had the eerie feeling that for a moment he was considering my offer in the light of what he was giving up. His stare disturbed me so thoroughly that I felt compelled to add, "Anything but life itself." In the rapid images emerging from the deeps of my being, I had glimpsed myself sacrificing my blood to a giant siphon pumping to Stimmes. Where do childish fears go? They stay with us, it seems. What would I sacrifice for Stimmes, a friend? I was being honest. Anything but life itself.

He laughed, the sound of distant sandpapering. "I would never ask for more," he said. "I will tell you precisely what I need, but first I have to explain that I'm presently in a strange financial position. God help me, this is not a touch. There's enough to pay the hospital bill. In fact, I've paid it in full. I've taken care of the mortuary and burial fees. In other words, this hellish business is paid for. But there's not much beyond that." He paused as if to catch his breath. "I have no worries about Elizabeth. She's more of your world than of mine. As you may remember, I have a son. I've seen him only once in the past twelve years. I want to take care of him."

His gaze fell to his hands. Then he looked up at me again. "For the past year I've been researching a book. I have several contracts for it. One is from *View Magazine*. It wants to run the entire book in three issues. That should be worth in the neighborhood of fifty thousand dollars. Brenther will then publish it in hard cover." Stimmes raised a hand in a noncommittal gesture. "I don't know what that's worth."

"What's the subject?" I asked.

"I prefer that you don't know until after I'm dead. The book is the reason I called you. The research is done. After I'm dead someone will have to be found who will finish it. I don't want to know who completes it. I despise most of the writers I know and read. I want you to find a writer. I don't want you even to think about one until I'm gone. I want your only consideration to be the amount of money that my son can derive from it."

"You say that there's no more research needed."

"All I needed is done. It's hard to tell for another writer."

"You don't want me to begin work on it now."

"Absolutely not. I want it to be my book for as long as I live. I don't even want to discuss it with you."

"Where's the research?"

"I've packed it away in cartons and have put them in the care of my lawyer."

I don't know how possible it is for a human being to bury his curiosity when given a mystery and told to have responsibility for its care. This was now frustration for me. I had gone as far with my questioning as I dared. Yet I wanted to know more. My respect—indeed my fears—for Stimmes' condition caused me to hold my peace and restrain my inquiry into the subject of his book.

I turned my eyes from him to the window, seeing the dirty dark lacework of autumn treetops and the gloomed buildings beyond, all pressed by the heavy sky. I could feel Morgan's eyes watching me. I thought his lips had a crooked smile, seen by my dim sideway vision.

"My lawyer will call you and give you the cartons. Then you can open them and see for yourself." He squinted his eyes and seemed to be laughing noislessly.

A transformation seemingly had taken place in Morgan's character. There had always been an arrogance about him, but it had always seemed to be a physical posture and an appearance rather than something meaningful in his behavior. His sense of superiority had never manifested itself in that meanest of human behaviors, the knowledge that one could manipulate other people. I didn't know how or why, but I was being used. I would not deny him a favor, and he must have known that. There was no question that I would agree to find a writer to finish his book.

At this moment I felt that Morgan had just fitted me for a specific role. It was as if he had decided with accuracy what my reactions might be in a given set of circumstances and had just wound up the spring that would release the situation. As I watched him laugh, listening to his airy hisses, I involuntarily shivered. I wished it were possible that he would not die and that I would not thereafter become involved. But I knew he would die and that I would be inextricably tied to whatever he had planned for me.

Death is an awkward matter for the living; its obligations are so many. I was in no position to argue with Morgan as I might have done had not death been present. I could not complain, for it would sound like the indigestive whines of a man bloated with feast in the company of the starving. While waiting for him to cease his laughter, I privately said to myself that Morgan Stimmes and death command. I will follow. It was a kind of futility.

Elizabeth entered the room carrying a silver platter upon which was a coffee setting, gleaming as nothing else in the room. She had briskly come, but now she stood and her face grew sad. Defenseless womanhood, here she was. For an instant only, I was befuddled.

"What can I do?" I asked.

Then I knew. The problem she faced was simply that of a place to set the coffee tray. What sort of a gentle background would have made her look so disconsolate over a simple and domestic chore? I rose quickly, even though she did not answer, and took the burden from her hands. All was grace again. I had had a maiden aunt who died at eighty-five when I was just a boy. She had been the only person I had ever known or seen who would have appeared to wilt under a similar problem. However, the moment I had removed her difficulty, I noticed with surprise that Elizabeth's face, as it turned from me, seemed to show contempt.

By retrieving the tray I had only created a problem for myself. Elizabeth, now absolved from responsibility, sat down in the wing-back chair near the fireplace and folded her legs beneath her as if she were a schoolgirl. I finally pushed a pile of magazines to the floor from the coffee table and put my charge down.

"No sugar or cream, thank you," she said, and then she turned to Morgan. "If you would, Morgan, I think Mozart would be just right with coffee in the morning."

Morgan's eyes narrowed. I bent over the coffee tray, wondering if he would finally rise. He did, but with great physical effort. He had not told me the effect of the cancer on his body, but now I saw it. He hacked for air, gulping it hungrily as he moved. His left side seemed restricted, as though the muscles there would not comply with his command of movement. This way he moved to the phonograph. I was suddenly aware that I had stopped my own action of pouring the coffee.

"Mr. Leeds, I think you're daydreaming," she said. She was looking at me, oblivous of her husband's painful effort.

Staring at Morgan, I wondered how she could be cruel enough to ask this of him. Doesn't she know? I asked myself. "Can I help you, Morgan?" I asked.

He stood for a moment, his teeth clenched, looking at me. He glanced at his wife. She was still watching me, her face showing annoyance.

"I think not," he said, and he leaned over the phonograph, clutching at its top, gripping each side until his knuckles turned white.

I caught my breath as he slowly raised the lid of the machine and with excruciating deliberateness lifted the records already in position and placed them in the rack. In the same sort of measured motion he removed two records and put them on the turntable. He twisted a knob and retired to his seat. There was still no music, only the rumbling sound of rotating disks.

I finally was able to pour coffee. Elizabeth was intently scanning my face. She was obviously walling in her impatience, her truculence. Her small lips pouted as those of a child might. Her color had heightened, a blush brushed across her fair ivory cheeks.

She abruptly turned toward her husband. "Morgan," she said, "I still don't hear Mozart." Her tone was that of a person who had suddenly decided that there was a plot to deny her.

Morgan closed his eyes. He began to rise, the painful trip about to be repeated.

I handed a cup of coffee to her. At that moment the phonograph began to play, shrieking forth with a screech of violins. I rushed to the phonograph, peering down into its spinning entrails.

"Morgan!" I heard her command. "Do something! He doesn't know what to do!"

I lifted the arm, ending the Mozart noise, leaving only an electronic buzz. I felt the desperation, the need to prove that I could solve this task before Morgan was compelled to move. "I've got it," I yelled, and I twisted dials until finally the background hum faded. Then I replaced the arm and there was Mozart music.

I whirled about, still agitated, still upset by her unreasonable behavior, and found Morgan still in his seat, lighting a cigarette unconcernedly, and Elizabeth with her head back, her skin back to ivory, her tightly doubled hands pressed against her chin, her eyes closed. She was the picture of reverie, a woman being bathed by music. Morgan winked at me.

Only I was left with the disturbance. My heart pounded. I wanted to explain my feelings, I want to condemn her for heartlessness and childishness. But it was all over. I had the uncomfortable feeling that if I were to speak, neither of them would understand what I was talking about.

I returned to the coffee table. I wondered if the fact that I had never married or lived with a woman for more than a week would explain my deep involvement with this small scene of domesticity and my inability to shrug it off as they had done.

"Sugar and cream," Morgan said.

Elizabeth opened her eyes. "I wish you would try to speak more naturally," she said. "You have such a lovely voice, Morgan." She closed her eyes again and leaned back into her aural bath. I was appalled and looked at Morgan for his reaction. He was smiling indulgently. For the first time I knew what he had meant when he told me that she would not accept the fact that he was dying. She not only would not accept it, she was determinedly living as though he were completely healthy. She was not permitting him self-pity or her mercy. She would not even permit him to have my mercy.

"There's no necessity to have an agreement, I think," Morgan said to me after I had poured my own coffee and sat down. "I've put you in my will as my literary executor. When I'm dead, you will simply do your duty."

Elizabeth was, I was surprised to see, ignoring us.

"I don't regard it as duty," I said . . . I was about to add that my friendship for him transcended words like duty, but realized that this entire matter had stuffed my head with unctuous sentimentality. Morgan would not have appreciated it. He knew of my friendship or he would not have called me.

We had once been to the funeral of a mutual friend and had left before the service was completely over. We had stood at the bar in silence, drinking, alone while together. He had turned to me finally. "You know," he had said, "only the bastards need the kind words at the end. I'd like to hear the truth just once." Grimly he had lifted his glass. "What the hell can an articulate man say about a friend's death? It's a fearful distance to go, but have a good trip." He had downed his drink and left.

"How long do you have left?" I asked. I was startled at my own bluntness, suddenly afraid that I had said something gauche, that my impulse to speak candidly was misplaced.

My fear was groundless.

"Death, you mean. My death," he said. He had not flinched. "I've been in a hospital for a month. I'm full of drains and holes. In two weeks I'm going back for x-rays. My doctor expects that I won't make it that far. I've been sent home to die, but I won't die here. Two weeks is no time at all. I can live that out easily. I won't have Elizabeth finding me dead." He nodded his shaggy head toward his wife. "Look at her. When I use the word death, she doesn't hear. If she does, she won't acknowledge it."

Elizabeth was listening to the concert. She was a beautiful gazelle of a woman entranced by melody.

"How will I know where to find your . . ." I stopped my question abruptly, stopping before saying the word "son." Morgan had pressed a finger across his lips to indicate he wanted my silence.

He studied Elizabeth for a second as though to be certain that she was not paying attention. He raised his hand horizontal to the floor to show size. It was clear that he knew that my question was about his son. I nodded.

"After I'm gone, you'll know," he said.

Elizabeth was sitting forward. Her eyes were open, and she was studying both of us. Morgan was smiling smugly.

An hour later, in a ragged, dark and dank bar on Eighth Avenue—an excavation and little more, clawed out of a brown-brick dirty wall of a building—I stood with a raw jigger of cheap whiskey in my hand. I had had death before; it had come into my family and had taken a mother and a brother. I had lost friends before, this way. Sometimes I had cried, for a mother and a brother. And sometimes I had felt alone, for friends (I was older then and less apt to cry). Now I felt nothing. If I felt anything, it was a sense of relief to be away from Morgan. I had discussed death as though it were part of a train schedule. (Are you leaving on the five-twenty or the six-ten? Say hello to my friends when you get there. Perhaps you'll meet my brother. Fine guy. Older than me. You'll both get along just fine.) I wondered if doctors develop this kind of detachment. I remembered one saying to me when my brother died, "It's a fact of life; accept it."

I said to the bartender, a wizened head full of wise wrinkles topped with a little hair, "Does Morgan Stimmes ever come in here?" It wasn't impossible, for Morgan used odd places for drinking.

"Can't say," the bartender said. "Does he live near here?"

"He's a writer. Maybe you've heard of him."

He scratched at his wrinkles. "Stimmes? Sure. I guess I haven't heard his name since the war."

I couldn't stand the idle talk any longer. I said what was on my tongue. "He's dying." I finally was relieved. This spare sentence uttered to a complete stranger had permitted me emotion. It's strange. I wanted desperately to feel grief. I was satisfied, however, to feel sorrow.

Three

I RETURNED TO THAT HUMDRUM WELL-ORDERED EXISTENCE at the university. I was a teacher, a Professor of Art. I tried to put Stimmes from my mind. It was impossible.

My impatience began the same afternoon after seeing Morgan. By the following day I felt overwhelmed by it. What was there that I could do for relief? Call Morgan by telephone? "Oh, you're still alive? Sorry. I'll try later."

It was not a good time of year to have a distraction. I was still struggling to identify all the young and golden faces of my students, wondering if any of them would stand out in my mind in the spring—to my dismay, I knew only two or three faces would and the rest would be lost. Morgan's plight intruded on everything I did.

One of my students—a nameless, faceless creature—stood up on the day after I returned from seeing Morgan and asked, "What about art that pictures death or dead things? Can it be beautiful?" I'm afraid I was stunned. I forgot entirely my train of thought and became for a moment engaged in a sort of retrospective trance with Morgan. He had once said to me, "It depends on how you die. With courage, one dies beautifully."

"What nonsense!" I said aloud to my class, just as I had once said to my friend. Necrophilia is one of the absurdities a man uses to contemplate his own decay, and I said something to that effect to the class, and the young man sat down and was instantly lost in the parade of young men. (God! How arrogant a professor can be! What he can get away with!)

I dismissed the class early and fled. I paused on the steps of Booth Hall and stared over the campus. The period bell had not yet rung, so the students wandering across that gray landscape were probably mine. I had another class late in the afternoon. I was free until then. There was no particular preparation for the later class, for it was for graduate students, and I allowed them to run their own incursions into aesthetics. (I often wondered how it was that I ended up at a small New England college teaching aesthetics, its philosophy. Unlike other people I was doing precisely what I had meant to do, even when trying to avoid it. I had written a small book on the more lurid aspects of Van Gogh's career on order from a publisher whom I had met at a cocktail party. A book on the same subject had done well some years before, and the publisher reasoned that another might be popular again if it were given a sufficiently lurid title. He called it *The Bloody Ear*. I was then writing a column on art for a New York newspaper. As result of publicity on the book, I received an offer to teach a course for an adult extension course on art appreciation, and accepted. As time passed, I became established in a career. The book, in the meantime, failed to sell more than a few thousand copies. So much for opportunistic publishers and my career.)

I sat down on the top step and breathed deeply of the chill air. I had two weeks to wait, I told myself. Somehow I believed Morgan that he would continue to live until he made it back to the hospital. I'm ashamed to admit that I almost wished it were over. Almost? There was no such qualification. Only a day had passed since I had seen him, but I had a cold impatience to have his death over with.

I was saved from the inevitable self-recriminations and self-directed anger for my heartlessness by the appearance of a student. Across the campus came a young girl—young? I imagine she was in her twenties—whom I recognized as being in my afternoon class. I didn't know her name and was barely able to differentiate her from the others except by the realization that she was one of the five female members of my class.

Oh yes, I recognized her as being one of those students who insist on lingering after the end of a class. I know that it's a weakness of my character, but when I had been in college, I had despised the breed who attempted to ingratiate themselves with their professors with after-class brightness. I continued to despise them.

As I saw her coming, I wondered which of the very few opening shots she would use that they always used when nearing their game. I dismissed "Do you think . . . ?" and "Don't you believe . . . ?" Both of these were reserved for the instant after class. This had to be an on-the-road greeting, such as "I love this weather, don't you?" or "Isn't the weather depressing?"

She said, her mouse face becoming long and serious, "I just heard the news that Morgan Stimmes is dying. He was a friend of yours, wasn't he, Professor Leeds?"

My reaction must have been startling to her, as her question had been to me. I said, rising from the step, "I can't imagine that it's any of your business." And I left her. I didn't ask her where she heard her news. I had taken quite a few steps before I turned and thought of asking the question. She was gone.

That evening, when I happened to be listening to a radio news broadcast, I learned that Morgan had been removed from his home and taken to a hospital. God knows why he was considered newsworthy. The radio news writer obviously did the best he could to make the announcement important. The report was loaded with reference to his past, and all of our pasts. It was as if Stimmes had been an anachronism in the modern age, the kind of person people note the existence of with the words "I thought he had died." It didn't seem curious to me that the report had found its way into the news media. Hospitals keep very efficient publicity men on their staffs for just such opportunities.

Even with my impatience earlier, I felt disappointed that Morgan had not made his two weeks. At least he was not going to die at home.

I attempted to telephone Elizabeth and was relieved to find that the Stimmes phone was not answered. I tried to reach her twice more than evening. Relief describes accurately my feelings as I hung up each time. However, I noted another emotion.

I dreaded speaking to her and having to utter the necessary words of condolence, realizing that she had not previously accepted the eventual early death of her husband. However, strangely, I wanted to hear her voice. I wanted to comfort her. I had a kind of raw desire to see her. Perhaps it was then, that evening, that I should have contemplated the subject of weakness. Weakness? Dear God! Was that what it was? I was permitting my affection for Morgan to fade. Was that because I was finding my affection for his wife increasing? From what I had seen of her, I should have a dread of her. Perhaps all that a man must do to meet the frustration of not being able to talk to some woman is to find her alluring. Alluring? Alluring enough to forget a friend?

The following morning, upon reaching my office, I found a letter. It was from Morgan.

When did he find the time and energy to write it? I wondered. As I tore it open, it occurred to me that he might have written it earlier and given it to his lawyer to send me when his final condition became sufficiently clear. The bulk of pages also convinced me that there was something official about the letter.

However, the date in the upper right-hand corner was that of the day I had seen him. And the date was underlined as was Morgan's inevitable way. I knew of no one else who emphasized time as he did.

> Dear Leeds,
>
> How delighted I was to see you. Please be seated. I know that you probably expected something more meaningful, more formal than this letter, and have ripped the envelope open and are still standing.

I smiled. Even in his last days he was shrewdly aware of reactions. I laid the letter on my desk sheepishly. Then I followed my daily routine. I had picked up a container of coffee on my way. Now I removed its cardboard top, putting in two cubes of sugar, rotating a wooden paddle in it. I strolled to the venetian blind and arranged the slats to capture the early morning sun. Consciously aware that I was delaying the reading of the letter, I was taking a childish pleasure in keeping it secret from myself, savoring the feelings I knew I would soon have. I always had appreciated letters from Morgan.

Finally, seated comfortably in my swivel chair, my warm coffee sipped slightly, I continued with the letter. There were voices humming from the corridor, but they seemingly faded as I read.

> No time for witty asides or vagrant notions. I simply want to explain Elizabeth. Explain? Pray for me that I can explain! Why the hell should I? I know why. I could sense your shock—or was it simply surprise? I've conjectured on my own sense of guilt. No help there. I've never felt guilt, so I wouldn't recognize it if I felt it. And when your insides are half gnawed away, how would a man recognize anything but the feeling of being eaten? (I've told my doctor that I can hear the cancer chewing when the night is both black and silent. He says that I can't.)
>
> I've known Elizabeth since she was a child. I was older. Let that be the end of that. You know my age. There is no way for me to put a number to her age. She's a woman.

She's a special sort of woman. I've never known another like her. She is as artless as a diapered babe and as knowing as the most common harlot—and as jaded and as disgusting. If I were not dying, I could never have written this much of the letter. I can only imagine what a Catholic feels during his confessional. What a strange religion to demand a weekly soul-wrench without benefit or the comforts of death soonest.

Who is Elizabeth? Her name before marriage to me was Elizabeth DeNane Passante Wester. I could give you the lineage of the center two names, but they are not American and are dull in the way of ancient Mediterranean families, too sun-baked, too fiercely frightened.

Do you remember Claude Wester? Marvelous man! A superb man! There was a time when the name Wester had meaning in this country, allied to the arts of patriotism and tradition.

The name Wester also had meaning for me. Obviously Morgan was alluding to meaning during an earlier age of American history. Claude Wester had certainly done a fine job of obliterating all fame the name had before him. Claude Wester began his career during the 1920's by promoting a Costa Rican Railroad Bond issue that turned out to be a swindle. And I knew that because my father had lost money on it. Wester escaped responsibility. I was depressed to read Morgan's descriptive summations: "marvelous," "superb."

I hope you won't completely judge him by the outcome of the Blassingfield-Imperial affair. He was a genius of finance and much misunderstood.

I laughed. I doubted if Claude Wester had ever been misunderstood, except possibly by Morgan.

Never heard of the Blassingfield-Imperial affair? I would think that was almost impossible except that I know you. It will annoy the hell out of you, but I won't explain beyond saying that Claude pocketed two million dollars and never returned to the United States.

I knew Claude during that period and visited him at his modest dwelling in France. I must emphasize the words modest and dwelling. He was terribly confused by the uproar that was raised over the Blassingfield-Imperial business and was hurt by the fact that he couldn't return here without facing prosecution, or threat of it, for his part. By his standards, he was living as a man lives doing penance. Had a trip to Canossa been open to him as it had to Emperor Henry IV, he, too, would have stood barefooted.

> However, by most standards, his home was palatial. And there I met Elizabeth, his only child.
>
> She was a plaything, a brittle miniature mannequin who, though young (she was not yet in her teens), preferred her place at the table and her seat at the salon to the doll house and the swing. I found her an entrancing demi-demoiselle. One difficulty that I've had in my marriage to her is the unshaken memory of her as a girl; it glooms our marriage bed. Perhaps there is guilt in me. I sometimes look at her, surprised that she is not straight-figured and breastless, and feel strangely uneasy.

I think that he attributed his uneasiness to the wrong cause. Without his past experience, I felt the same sort of surprise that she was entirely adult. There was still something of his "demi-demoiselle" about her.

There were several pages of the letter that dealt with the passage of time, and Morgan's means of passing time was no brief expository matter. He plodded paragraph after paragraph in explanation of how he passed that time. Always an interesting writer, he was a master of being fascinating even when practicing circumlocution.

He startled me with one passage. It came with succinct directness after the wartime moments.

> All of the dinosaurs are dead now or have undergone metamorphosis into people, except me. That's apropos of absolutely nothing but my internal musing. Lonely, eh?

Sunshine flicked the windshield of a passing automobile and darted across my office, catching my attention in the same manner that Morgan's aside caught my mind. He had parenthesized his tragedy as a human being. I wasn't certain that he fully understood what he had written. If he understood, Morgan Stimmes was the stuff of classical tragedy. Perhaps I've become something of a pedagogue, but the sight and sound of a modern man who runs pell-mell to his inevitable doom, knowing what drives him, excites me.

It's too pat to pigeonhole any person, but there was an absurd truth about Stimmes' likeness to a dinosaur in character. As one of the young men, in 1927, who helped to create *View Magazine* and, subsequently, a publishing empire, he roared and ranged over the green world, pasturing hungrily. Was it responsible journalism he practiced? I'm not certain it was journalism. It was optimism. Not simple unadorned optimism either. It was beautiful and wonderful, fixing firmly on a world that had reached its brightest apex. He wasn't alone then. The young men who began *View* and its offshoot enterprises were seemingly of one mind.

I can remember reading *View* after the Depression had begun. These were the young men who took the antique American spirit of competitiveness and gave new meaning to "First," "Most," "Biggest," "Tallest," "Smallest." The Depression was almost instantly described as "Great" and the two words were capitalized of course. It was during the "Great Depression" that Stimmes first began to lose his way. The style of journalism wasn't gone, for bread lines were described individually as the "longest"; and Stimmes continued to thrive. He once told me that he had never earned less than twenty thousand dollars a year until—and "until" is the important word—the war was over.

He was suddenly a man who wore a derby and spats among the newly fashioned, except that with him it was something internal. It wasn't a heroic world any more. Even the superlatives of *View Magazine* became fewer, and when they appeared they were often qualified with a doubting phrase, such as "one of the most."

Given sometimes to phrases that border on the pompous, I hesitated, while reading Morgan's letter, to be as pompous as I might. It was too simple. American had matured and Morgan had not.

I went back to the letter.

When I saw her again, many harsh things had happened to her. Her father was dead and the house had been gutted by fire during the war. That's a yarn in itself, and I regret that I will never be able to sit with you over a warming glass and spin it for you. There was no reason for me to pity her and I didn't. Ask her where the money went and you'll understand. She was capable of living under any and all circumstances.

I had parachuted into southern France with two American Intelligence agents. To my everlasting shame I lost them. In the lovely village of Carmaux, I finally dared to ask for a glass of port of an old farmer. Port he did not have, but he did have a nutty red wine in his cellar and Elizabeth in his kitchen. I would never have recognized her. I was surprised to see a young woman in his kitchen who was as comely as she. The French farmer, as a rule, has the rather ancient notion that women are domesticated working creatures who are happily shaped so as not to incur the Church's wrath on the subject of sodomy . . .

Elizabeth recognized me. I was delighted, of course, to

see her. The farmer was not happy that I was delighted. My stop there was brief. With her as a guide (and the farmer's provisions in my sack), I made the perilous journey southward over the Pyrenees into Spain. It's astonishing that I use the word "perilous," for it was not that, apparently. I thought it was for a time. Something in me resents any exploration into that month, even by myself.

I went to England and Elizabeth stayed in Spain. I recreated the original Elizabeth. I have, over the years, financially supported this reeducation. We wrote one another letters over the space of years. I felt rather good about her. It was a noble enterprise I had embarked upon, the resuscitation of ideals in a woman who was shorn of them by the damned necessities of life. She lived comfortably and quietly with the Family Cifuentia in a marvelous whitewashed villa outside of sun-washed Valencia.

The Stebbins visited her two years ago. You remember the Stebbins! Phil is a skinny cuss with a twitch over his right eye.

Phil was so taken with Elizabeth that he tried to convince me that I should permit her to leave Spain and become his invalid daughter's companion. As usual, he had incorrectly appraised the situation. Elizabeth had always been free to make her own choices. She was happy to stay and to continue to accept money from me. (There is always some bitterness in a man who contracts either willingly or otherwise to support a young woman.)

The Stebbins told me that they had never seen a lovelier young woman nor a more sensitive one. I had purposefully stayed away from her all those years. Her letters were warmly affectionate, as a daughter's might be to a father. What more is there to say? I was beguiled by her. Her innocence flowered again and grew strong. And one day the letters stopped coming from her. I wrote her more frequently than ever. Each time I pleaded with her to write. I ordered her to write me. I stopped the money. Still no word! The Family Cifuentia became upset; and I learned from the many members of that family—father, mother, uncles, and aunts flooded my mailbox—that she had decided not to write me again and that no amount of cajolery or threats would change her mind. I flew to Spain. And we were married.

On that short sentence, the letter ended. Morgan's signature whirled across the lower page in lovely indecipherable loops. I leaned back and picked up my coffee—my forgotten coffee—and drank it cold.

Then I tried to call Elizabeth again. There was no answer. When I hung up, I understood, to some degree, Morgan's concern about the absence of letters.

Four

IN THE SOLITUDE OF MY OWN APARTMENT, LISTENING without concentration to the background noise of my radio, I pattered about, forgetting my loneliness. Then I heard the eleven o'clock news.

"Morgan Harper Stimmes, one of the Second World War's great correspondents, died this evening, two days after being admitted to a hospital for cancer."

And that was that. Then the weather report followed. I had just lit a cigarette, having pulled down the spread on my bed, and began the walk from the tiny bedroom across the slightly larger than tiny sitting room to the minute kitchen—a few steps describing my entire apartment. I halted and puffed contemplatively on my cigarette. I accepted the news with neither sadness nor relief. I was almost more preoccupied by the jargon of the weather report than by the reality of Morgan's death. I had expected either sadness or relief, and in that sense I suffered a mild disappointment. I think I might have continued across the living room to complete my original intention of making myself a cup of instant coffee, undressed and settled myself warmly under covers with a book, but the telephone rang just then.

"Mr. Leeds?"

"Yes."

"I know that this is a terrible imposition for me to call you, but Morgan died. I don't know any of his friends except you. I won't be able to sleep tonight. Would you come to New York and keep me company? I beg of you not to refuse . . . Please." Elizabeth's voice was taut, higher in pitch than I remembered.

Having finally found a parking space for my car, and feeling a degree of haste because of the time it took me to reach her apartment, I rang the doorbell—received a buzz, which opened the door—and used the rickety elevator.

What impulse was it that strummed inside of me? Even then I realized that I had a plaintive need for a woman, that I had desires which had been vaguely aroused by my inability to talk to her two days earlier. But an erosion had taken place.

It had taken me two hours to reach New York that night. And I had suffered the hypnotic weariness of facing a continuous stream of headlights and following a line of pin-sized bumper red lights. And I had thought of grief. If I had had grief to suffer over Morgan . . . Memory of my emotions of death was a pale substitute. I had spent most of my trip trying to memorize phrases of comfort for Elizabeth. Perhaps I had been too prepared for this death to feel it with sorrow. All I could do was attempt to understand Elizabeth's shock.

She had left the apartment door ajar, so I knocked and entered. There was no sign or sound of her. In my first quick glance in the hallway, as I called out for her, I saw that a transformation had taken place in just the corridor. The mirror had been cleaned and its frame polished. A series of small gay watercolors, encased in creamy white borders, were now on the wall. Even the strip of carpet running down the hall was new. I put my topcoat on the hall chair and hesitated.

"Come into the living room, Mr. Leeds," she said distantly, oddly without the tones of anguish or tension, unlike her voice on the telephone.

A fire was in the fireplace, and little licks of flame ate a wide log. A smudgy gray smoke rose along the draft. Along the rear of the mantel, a parade of small tiles leaned but seemed to have motion. Each had a simple design, glazed of burning colors. These provided almost a reflection of the fire below.

"I've made a few changes," she said. I turned to look at her, having missed her when first entering. I had even wondered where her voice had come from. She sat where Morgan had sat the last time I had seen him, and I remembered him.

"I didn't really think he was going to die," she continued. "I know he said he was, but sometimes he said . . ." She hesitated. "He said so many things that were not necessarily true." Her face was colorless. I had always assumed that a woman's lips had color beneath the cosmetic. Hers were only a shade darker than her white skin.

"Please sit down and we'll talk." With such simple grace she removed the necessity of more words.

"I came as quickly as I could. I'm sorry it took me so long."

She was smiling faintly. Her arms were drawn up, her fingers touching her face. "You're forgiven. I've been busy with the apartment. A woman needs something to do, you know. How awkward this must be for you! We barely know one another."

"I wanted to help earlier. I called you," I protested.

She glanced away briefly. "When Morgan went to the hospital, I moved into a hotel room. I didn't want to talk to anyone. I wanted to be alone." Then she fixed her eyes on me. She seemed to be studying me, as if measuring my disappointment. "I'm sorry," she added.

"I'm not sure I can be of much help now. Are there any arrangements I can make? I know Morgan said he had done everything humanly possible to foresee all the eventual problems."

"He made things extremely simple," she said bitterly. She looked down at her hands, which were now interlaced as in hard prayer. "I saw him yesterday for fifteen minutes, and he said good-bye. I won't even see his remains." She looked up. Her eyes widened. She herself seemed startled by what she had just said. "I didn't mean that I wanted to. I have no wish to see . . ."

"It's all right. I understand." Even as I spoke I wondered if she were not still holding a belief that Morgan was still alive.

She sighed, as if relieved of the necessity of explaining further. There was a silence between us suddenly. What could I say? Nothing seemed appropriate. I searched my mind for a subject, but I could only think of Morgan. It was not an occasion to dredge forth memories, not at least until she showed a desire to hear eulogies of her husband.

"He wrote you a letter, didn't he?" she suddenly asked.

I showed surprise inadvertently. It was not because I was surprised. She must have known that he had written someone. I was surprised only in the sense of being startled that she did not know for certain that Morgan had written me. She was guessing.

"He didn't?" She had taken my silence for a denial.

I considered the content of the letter and decided that it was meant only for my eyes. I would be embarrassed to have to refuse her if she wanted to see it.

"If he did, I'm afraid I haven't received it."

"I wonder to whom he wrote. I was positive it was you."

She rose from her seat and walked resolutely to the fire, bending, leaning as though to see it. She was wearing a black dress embroidered with raised weltlike stitches. Its collar was a series of folds, and she looked as if she were a silhouette of a flower still a bud. She finally turned toward me. "I've done nothing but embarrass you."

As I began to protest, she shook her head. "I want to apologize," she said. She smiled quickly. "I'm sure you know almost nothing about me. Hasn't Morgan written you before about me?"

I remembered Morgan telling me that he had told her that he had. "On several occasions, very briefly, mostly about his love for you."

Her look hardened as if she knew that I was lying. Then her eyes twinkled mischievously. "Did he really write that to you? How very sweet of him! I have so many carbons of his letters to others. I haven't been through all of them, of course, but I never found one addressed to you. Perhaps his letters to you were of a more personal nature." She paused, and then asked offhandedly, "You aren't a homosexual, are you?"

I had never been asked to answer a question such as that one before. Again I was speechless, trying to fathom the reason for her question.

"You aren't, are you?" she repeated.

"No, I'm not," I said, stunned.

"I'm glad," she said. "I really didn't think so." It was as though my answer erased the topic. She had an astonishing facility for lurching from subject to subject. To her it was a painless ability; however, she left me gasping, contending with the repercussive memory of those things she so easily dismissed. "I hope I haven't disappointed you in the amount of grief I display. I loved Morgan very much. I spent the last few days weeping. I don't think I can shed one more tear. They're all gone. Can you understand that?"

I said that I understood, but I didn't. Even at my age, caught up with the image of my mother or my brother, I have found that I could still cry. Perhaps there's self-pity in lonely moments, and I've had many of those. And then, perhaps self-pity has nothing to do with grief.

"You don't have to console me. I should think you would be pleased that you don't have to spend an evening with a weepy female."

"I just want to help." For a fairly articulate human being, I found myself trapped into insipid replies.

"You must be very tired."

I glanced at my watch involuntarily. It was almost two in the morning. "Not very," I said. "If you regret asking me to come, just say the word. I won't be offended."

She shook her head emphatically.

"Are there any things left to do?" I asked. "Are there funeral preparations?"

"All arranged. Morgan has even taken care of the services and the announcements. I imagine you'll receive one in the mail tomorrow, or soon. I don't even know who to thank for sending them. He's being cremated, you know. A few friends have been invited to the chapel across the park."

"I imagine his lawyer took care of that."

"I don't think so. Yesterday he was very upset with his lawyer. I don't know why. All I know is that Morgan canceled his original agreement with him, or said he did."

A thunderclap should have sounded. It was then I realized that she had called me to New York for some purpose other than having a person to pass the time with. With casual conversation she had announced that my link with the dead Morgan had been broken. There was no lawyer any more who would bind me to my promise to Morgan.

"What's the lawyer's name?" I asked lamely.

"I don't know." She smiled wanly.

How was it possible that she didn't know? I couldn't utter the doubts I felt. She entrapped me in frustration.

"A young man came this evening and brought several cartons," she continued. "I knew that Morgan had been preparing to write a book. He was very secretive about his work. Soon after he became ill, he packed everything and took it out of the apartment." She studied me. She parted her lips, and her teeth were clenched. "Do you like me?" she asked finally. That easily she moved on.

What other answer could I give? "Of course. I only met you once before tonight, but I trust Morgan's judgment about people." It was my turn to smile. "I think you were, by far, the best choice he had made of all his wives."

She thrust her head back and began to laugh explosively.

For a moment I tensed, wondering if she had become hysterical. Her laughter pealed and resounded in the quiet room.

"Oh, dear God," she said, finally. "I deserved that."

"I meant it as a compliment."

"I'll take it as one then. I forgive you for my own sensitiveness. I didn't really mind. I was wondering if I could laugh again. And I did." Then she walked toward me. "May I call you Leeds? Morgan always did, and I know you by that name. I would prefer if you call me Elizabeth." She leaned down and kissed me on the forehead. That strange perfume seemed to rise from her body like a vapor. She stood straight again. "There," she said, "we're friends now. You're my friend. Morgan's dead, and you and I are friends." She bit the tip of her tongue contemplatively. "Follow me."

I rose in doglike obedience and followed. There was nothing for me to say. We went down the hallway. She stopped at a closed door. "Forgive me the wiles of a woman," she said. "The cartons are in here."

I laughed, the sound of hesitant embarrassment. The wiles of a woman? I was perhaps more susceptible to them, than most men. Even under the guilt of being alone with the widow of a former friend, I had begun to suspend my guards, had even considered my limping frame, my face as possibly appealing. She had enwrapped me with the gauze of her perfume, had kissed me, had called me a friend.

She seemed to realize. "I'm sorry," she said. "I couldn't possibly tonight. Perhaps sometime." Then she opened the door and pointed to the cardboard cartons. "There they are." She was a child showing off a present.

"Do you know what's in them?" I was learning to accept her swift change of conversation and emotion.

"I just opened one," she said. "There's a letter addressed to you. He must have written it when he packed the carton. It's dated August." She added brightly, "I read it. It's not very informative." She tugged back the top and snatched the letter from the pile of papers.

"Leeds," it said succinctly under an August 10 date. *"This is it. Good luck. I wish I could be with you. Morgan."*

"What does it mean?" she asked.

I explained my agreement to serve as his literary executor. "It wasn't supposed to be quite like this. Morgan told me that I'd get them from a lawyer."

"Does this change anything?"

"I guess it doesn't. I promised him. Did he say anything about it?" I was mystified, and my concern probably showed on my face.

"I was very upset. He apparently had contacted this lawyer—I wish I knew his name—and wanted to change his instructions. There was something about a child. Did Morgan have a child?"

"Didn't you know?"

"No."

"As I understand it, Morgan hadn't seen him in some years."

"I wish I had known."

I wondered what difference it would have made to their relationship.

"Do you know what the book is about?" I riffled through some of the manuscripts. At a cursory glance it was not possible for me to decide on the subject.

"My father," she said. "Didn't you know?" She stepped back. Her eyes were luminous, wide. Then she closed them, and when her eyes were open again, they were all business. "Morgan never told me, but he questioned me at length. I know he talked to some friends of my father's. He used to disappear into his study after he talked to me and type for hours. Sometimes, at one or two in the morning, he would come out and behave very strangely. He seemed to go into fits of depression. In a kind of anger he would stalk up and down the living room and then he would stop and glare at me. He wouldn't speak. He'd just stare. I would ask him what was wrong and he wouldn't answer. Finally, he would go to the kitchen and pour himself a drink, usually a tall one without ice. Then he would come back here. He'd stand in front of the fireplace and drink the entire glass down. Then he'd go to bed. On the nights this happened, he slept restlessly, tossing and turning."

"Did he ever say anything."

"Once or twice. I remember once he said that he missed the old days."

I could close my eyes and see Stimmes again. I could almost hear him pacing. I had only seen him once that way but that was on a better day. Or was it? I once had an apartment on the upper East Side. That area of the city had become popular some years before I moved there, but the Third Avenue El was still standing in its hulking array of blackened steel. The El was part of my life, for the train still ran then. I was able to have a fashionable address with an unfashionable apartment. The entrance to the building was on the side street, but my front window was a view for the El passengers.

I had just moved and was standing in the vacancy of the living room, surrounded by my crates of books. I was filled with the depression that must overcome all people moving; it has always visited me.

"You can't live here." I had instantly recognized the voice. Morgan was standing behind me.

"I'm going to. I am already living here."

"I won't let you."

I laughed sourly.

His eyebrows were crinkled in distaste. "How much can you afford a month?"

"I guess I can go as high as eighty. I'm paying sixty for this, and it's rent-controlled."

"Your phone isn't in?"

"Not yet."

"Don't let them move in any more. I'll be gone fifteen minutes at the most, just time enough for a few phone calls. I'll find you something decent. I have a few friends who own buildings. Be patient, Leeds. I won't be long."

It was pointless to argue; he was gone so quickly. However, I should have made an attempt to stop him. I had been a month finding that apartment, having lost my other to a private building development. I could have had an apartment in the new development, but I would have had to accept a one-room, with a kitchen on the wall, and pay more than a hundred dollars in rent.

Morgan's commanding blond optimism was infectious; he made me hopeful. When the moving man appeared, I gave him five dollars and told him to take his partner and have a few beers on me.

When Morgan reappeared, I knew that my hopefulness had been misplaced. He strode up and down my apartment, his shoes smacking angrily as he went.

"No luck?"

"I'm going out to have a drink," he had answered. "Join me?" His face was severe, his eyebrows still a peaked roof of concern.

* * *

Elizabeth ducked her head into the carton. "I'm just dying to read everything here. I really didn't know much about my father's business affairs."

I remembered Morgan's letter. "Did you know about the Blasingfield-Imperial Affair?" I asked.

She stood erect again and searched out my eyes with hers. Her eyelids closed partially as she stared at me suspiciously. "I've heard of it," she said. "There was a period in my life when my father talked of nothing else. However, that wasn't what he called it, that's Morgan's name for it." Then she closed the lid of cardboard. "If you want to take the cartons with you, I'll need some kind of written statement from you that lists the contents. Perhaps it would be better if I kept them. I must protect myself."

"If I'm going to find someone to write the book, I'll have to explain the virtues of the project. I'm afraid I'll have to read a good part of it." I wasn't looking forward to reading any of it. "I'm going to have to find the contracts and then talk to the *View* people and the publisher."

"I have the contracts in a separate envelope. I want you to have them. I'd be interested in knowing how much I can earn out of this." She smiled. "I don't really need the money," she said quickly.

I had had a problem in speaking frankly with Morgan that last time and now I had another equally touchy one. Having no idea of how to approach the subject of Morgan's request to me that the proceeds of any arrangement I made go to his son, I kept my peace. To talk of death to a dying man was difficult, and had been difficult with Morgan, but I found it impossible to say to his widow that he wanted no money to go to her. Had Morgan changed his mind at the last minute?

"Did Morgan leave any correspondence? I'd like to talk with his lawyer."

"Of course he did. I told you that he did." This was an edge of sharp temper. Did she think I was trying to trap her?

"Did you notice any letters to or from his lawyer?"

"I don't know why you want to speak to him. Morgan canceled all his arrangements. I've told you that."

"I just want to know what the arrangements were. I'd also like to know who his agent was." I was being as firm as I dared.

"I'll look if you like." It was a reluctant surrender, and I knew that it was probably meaningless. Unless I was able to see Morgan's correspondence, I'd have to devise another way of finding my information. I dreaded having to talk to the lawyer. I had the feeling that Elizabeth had not told me the truth. And if I was right, I was faced with confronting her with her lie.

She was looking into the other cartons now. Kneeling, she eagerly tore off the gummed tape. She had small breasts, but her position bunched them, and when she leaned her head back to say that the box held recording tapes, she caught me staring. "You poor man. I can make you blush very easily, can't I?" She stood again and watched my embarrassment. "You're very different from Morgan. He was very prudish outwardly. He'd never stare. However, he'd never blush." As if that moment had no significance, she kneeled again next to the box. "I wonder if these have Morgan's voice. I loved his voice. Let's see. Here's one that is just marked with the number one." Her pale face was flushed with excitement. Even her body seemed to participate; she writhed with joy. "You know where Morgan's study is. It's off the living room. There's a tape recorder there. You put it in the living room. There's a plug by the bookcase." She hugged the tape to her bosom. "I'll go and put some coffee on." She hesitated. "Would you prefer whiskey?"

"No," I answered.

I had no business being there. I remembered Morgan and my duty to him. Perhaps he was right; she was someone to beware of. It wasn't love, I told myself. I simply wanted. I damned the restrictions that a civilized education and upbringing had imposed on me. I even damned the bounds that my loyalties to Morgan made me suffer.

"Is it set up yet?" Elizabeth's elated question came from the kitchen.

"Not yet." I was achingly conscious of my slowness and then of my limp as I walked carefully with the recording machine into the living room.

"Hurry." She rushed in and watched me put the machine down and struggle with the cord. "You're very slow."

Involuntarily I sighed.

She laughed. "I'll be patient." She handed me the spool of tape. "Don't you dare start it before I come back." And she was gone with a leap.

Reflecting on my lack of tiredness, I wondered about the grace of God in giving me the inability to woo a woman and keep her. I had too often pursued one and been rejected to believe that I might some day succeed. But my very wakefulness meant to me that Elizabeth had given me belief.

"All ready to go!" I shouted. Why was I being triumphant?

"Hush, there are neighbors." She appeared holding that same tray which had provided me a problem only days before.

I rushed forward and took it from her. For an instant we both held it, our hands on opposite sides. She smiled thinly, knowingly, and then relinquished it.

"Are you there, Leeds? I've just returned from my first exploratory operation and I'm oozing excrement from a hole in my side. I stink to high heaven. I'm going to insist that they connect my intestines again."

I looked at Elizabeth. She was, as on the first morning I saw her, absorbing the sounds, this time Morgan's deep lilting speech. The meaning seemed to be gone; she was hearing only the music of his voice.

"This may seem to be a voice from the grave, for I'm dead now. Better make that a voice from the urn. I'd prefer it that way. I think I'll make that arrangement. Shall I have my ashes scattered? Where? It doesn't make a damn bit of difference. I'm straying."

Suddenly Morgan burst into a fit of laughter, manic in nature and sound. And it finally came to an end with gasps of breathlessness.

"He has a lovely voice," Elizabeth said, not opening her eyes. "And a fine laugh," she added.

I didn't answer.

"I'm sorry for that, Leeds," Morgan's electronic voice continued. "I'm not yet accustomed to the thought of death. I don't feel it, though I sure can smell it. That's not a joke based on what I said earlier. I can smell something different about my body. It's very much like the subtle aroma of a blue mold. Neither here nor there. I'm wandering. Give me a microphone and I wander.

"Listen to me, Leeds. This is important. Elizabeth . . ."

And then there was no Morgan. The two wheels of the player spun. I could hear the sounds of a room, the shuffling of feet, the movement of furniture. I heard an automobile horn in the distance.

Elizabeth opened her eyes. Her bloodless lips showed annoyance. "I hope that hasn't happened to the other tapes. He never seemed to understand how to operate that machine."

"It may come on again," I said hopefully. We sat, sipping our coffee, for the full play of the reel, and there was nothing but the vague suggestions of a room, the flickers of machine stridulation—as though a grasshopper were scraping. Every now and then I received the impression that a person was being recorded in almost silent movements. There were footsteps. I could hear a window being opened and then closed. These may have been imaginary, for I was straining to listen and cataloging everything in terms recognizable.

"It's useless," she said. And she rose and strode to the recorder and turned it off.

"Have you played it before?" I asked.

She faced me. "You're suspicious of me."

"Why should I be suspicious?"

"I don't know. But I've sensed it ever since you came. It doesn't please me, Leeds." The firelight brightened one side of her face, painting a second color—a wash of orange—across her cheeks. It heightened her exasperation. "It doesn't matter to me whether Morgan chose you to have his book finished. I can change all that. I can tell you to leave right now. I wouldn't see you again. If you do as I tell you, we could have a very agreeable relationship. If not, we're not going to have any."

I was caught off guard. I hadn't expected to be the accused. I sat and remained silent. I had no answer to give. Never lowering my eyes from her, seeing the whole woman—the breasts tucked neatly beyond view and defiantly rigid, the narrow waist, the shapely legs—I was hung between my pride and promise to Morgan and my need for her. Finally, "I don't have any suspicions. I don't understand what you mean."

"You're on my side, then?"

"What other side is there?"

"Good."

It was after four o'clock when I left Elizabeth. I had no material for the book with me. She had asked me to come back the next evening, Friday, and spend the weekend. She said she thought I could accomplish all the reading I'd find necessary during that time. I drove back along the early morning road with the lumbering trucks in procession, and could not forget the promise of her words "Perhaps sometime." I had not forgotten Morgan, but I buried him deep.

A nap is an unsatisfactory method of relieving the appetite for sleep. How is it possible to depict emptiness except with terms that have identity with hard sides and real shapes? My tiredness was a towering emptiness.

Haggard, I returned to New York. However, I went early. I was making a gesture to Morgan, a slight bow to his memory and my promise to him. I knew a young man at Brenther's and had called him. Perhaps it was my state, perhaps it was my guilt, but I had made an urgent plea to see him that afternoon, and he reluctantly agreed.

He was in his early thirties. Oh God, I hate young men in their early thirties! They know so much so well. I wonder why it was that Morgan never hated me when I was that age. There's another virtue! Morgan was an indulgent man and never hated those who trod behind him.

I sat for fifteen minutes in the outer hall of Brenther's before the receptionist managed to reach Boyd Hall's secretary. ("It'll be a few more minutes. Make yourself comfortable.") At a quarter of five (a half-hour later) a trim young lady opened the door to the inner recess and said, "Mr. Leeds, Mr. Hall will see you now."

Publishers' offices have always surprised me. The majority of those that I've seen have the look of being temporary, flung into operation for a gypsy moment, prepared to be moved the next. That may be a personal reaction, for the general disorder, the piles of books, the yellowing anxious faces passed in the hall remind me of the times I have moved from one apartment to the next.

Off a long pale-green corridor, in an office with a window, I found Boyd Hall. I had met him only two years earlier at the University during a dinner party. On several occasions we had had drinks together in New York. His dark eyes gleamed at the mention of names. I had once thought that his interest was people, that he was broadly involved in humanity and wanted to know who else there was. I had once become soggy with martinis and had laughed and suggested that he might spend some time with the phone book. "I don't give a damn about people," he had said, affronted. "I'm pumping you about people to find out if you know anyone who might produce a book." I find it uncomfortable to have a friend or a potential friend bluntly state that he has some opportunistic reason for being your friend, regardless of how slight that reason is.

He was in his shirt sleeves, necktie tugged loose; his greeting was perfunctory and crisp. "I haven't much time, Ken, what did you want to see me about?"

"Mind if I sit down?"

"Grab a seat." He looked down at the pile of papers in front of him, as though my visit with him would consist of my sitting down for a minute while he continued work.

"I want to discuss Morgan Stimmes' contract with Brenther. I thought you might be able to tell me whom I could talk to . . ."

"Oh yeah, you mentioned something about it on the phone. I hope you realize that I'm not in a position to discuss the company's business."

"I thought I explained that Morgan wanted me to be his literary executor."

"Did you?" Surprise. He arched his eyes. "Are you?"

I felt the pain of belittlement and also the lack of proper credentials. I was making a border crossing without a passport. My physical condition was not helpful in keeping a front. "Were you Morgan's editor here? I'm not trying to pull anything. I just need some information before I take on this assignment. Until last night I didn't even know what Morgan had been writing about."

Hall, my border guard, was obdurate. "I'd like to help you, Ken, but you see my position."

"No, I don't."

"For crying out loud! It's clear enough. Sure we had a contract with Stimmes. It's just no longer in force. He died. I can't discuss it with you until we make a decision about whether we want to go ahead on the book. Frankly, it's not my book, and I was against making the arrangement in the first place. And we wouldn't have agreed to sign a contract if Stimmes hadn't made that arrangement with *View Magazine*. Stimmes was once a good journalist, but hell, fashions change. He didn't."

"Who is his agent?"

"Stimmes have an agent? Are you kidding? He didn't believe in them."

"How about his lawyer? Do you know his name?"

"What the hell kind of literary executor are you if you don't know his lawyer? How the hell would I know?"

"Who is his editor here?"

"Not me, thank God."

"I'd like to talk to him."

"I'll tell him."

I stood up to go. I must have looked beaten, for his eyes softened; he looked sympathetic for the first time. He rose quickly and pressed my shoulder. "Sit down, Ken, you caught me on a bad day. Forgive me."

I sat down.

He smiled. He picked up the phone. "Let me speak to Teagarten." He winked. "George . . . I have a friend of mine in the office, and he's sort of unofficial literary executor for the Stimmes estate. He's trying to preserve the original contract . . . Yes, sir, I told him that. I'll have him get in touch with you by mail. Right. Thank you." He leaned over the cradled phone thoughtfully, pursing his lips, looking vacantly over my head. Then, as though dismissing a reverie, he fell back into his chair. "That was the boss. He wants you to know that the contract automatically ended when Stimmes died. He wants to give the matter some thought before seeing you. If you want to keep the pot boiling, I think you ought to see the boys at *View*. I'd lay money on it that our interest in the book would be dependent on *View*'s going ahead on it first. That kind of prepublication stimulates sales."

"All I really wanted to know was the name of Morgan's lawyer."

"Can't help you there."

With the futility born of tiredness, and a smoldering resentment at the treatment Hall had given me, I plodded to Fifth Avenue in order to take a bus to the Village. It's difficult for someone who has lived in New York to escape to the classification of being a stranger. The familiar, the frenzy, the mood—how brooding and sad that city can be even with its callithumpian marketplace agitation—bore into the very pores of the skin. In the space of a few blocks, I became a resident once more. I bustled with the bustlers and elbowed with the elbowers.

By five-thirty, when I walked off the bus at Eighth Street and Fifth Avenue, I had lost my hostility to Hall and my concern about Stimmes. Almost light-heartedly I swung my dispatch case—filled with toilet items, shirts and pajamas.

And into the park and among the trees and people

deadened by autumn I walked, feeling a vague disappointment that it was too late to see children. They would have been more in keeping with my growing exultation. There are probably no children who could have raced or played with enough glee to reflect properly my emotions of that moment. My earlier exhaustion had given my renewed joy in being in New York a special acuity; even my sense of smell sharpened and I appreciated the sweet-sour industrial scent of the city as it melted in the evening odor of park earth and rotting leaves. It was the aroma of a lascivious woman saturating in love. Perhaps I was meant for this city.

My conversation with Hall had released me somewhat from my obligation, for I had tried to satisfy Morgan's wishes. I was also relieved of worry about the long-term prospects of the book. At Brenther, at least, the book's status was shaky. What I had taken so seriously the previous night had become insubstantial and of secondary interest. I was now devoted to the enlarging reality of spending a weekend in the same apartment with Elizabeth. I understood that I would be a toy to her whims, but my swelling male egotism gave me dusty corners of fantasy. As I mounted the steps of the staircase, permitting myself the additional time of phantom thoughts and their sweet taste, forbidding myself the headlong rush and the dangers of the creaky elevator, I even convinced myself that I possessed unknown virtues. Certainly Morgan Stimmes had never had them. How fantastic the mind is when it spins the intricate passions of desire and creates goodness from evil and permits the evil to be performed!

As I rang the doorbell to the apartment, I wondered if she and I were going to have dinner at home or if we would go to a restaurant? It was an absurdity.

She opened the door and took my hand. "I thought you might be earlier," she said. She had a touch of color on her lips and a flicker of excitement in her eyes. "Quickly," she commanded, pulling me down the hall toward the living room. "I've arranged all the material and have set up the tape recorder. I met a friend today. Isn't that a remarkable coincidence? She's from Spain. She and I are having dinner together. I'm late. I hope you don't mind. I don't know when I'll be back." I watched, my eyes glazed, and she ran away from me, picking up a coat—a dark fur in a dark passage—opening a door, closing a door. I was alone in a dim-lit room massed with piles of papers.

* * *

I closed my eyes and listened to the tape. It was another room, somewhere in the city. A telephone rang and was answered by a stranger. "Sure, Lex, I can make it. Can't talk now." With pride the rusting voice said, "I'm being interviewed now by Morgan Stimmes. He's doing a book on Claude Wester. Maybe I'll have him call you. You knew Claude. Say, Morgan, you want to learn about Claude's college days. I've got Lex Treat on the phone."

"I was going to write him."

"He says he'll get in touch. See you tomorrow."

Click.

I hadn't eaten dinner. As if to combat my disappointment with Elizabeth's going, I had pitched into the pile of correspondence. I chose the wrong package to begin with, for it contained nothing but the early introductory letters, outlining the project—"a comprehensive study of a man who typified a stunning period of time." In an effort to fasten my attention on this work, I finally gave up the letters and turned to the record player, hopeful that it would give me enough information. I turned out the lights and fell back in a chair.

Click.

"Listen, I don't want any phone calls. I'm being interviewed and I want a clear hour."

Click.

"Sorry, Morgan. I think we'll have a little peace now."

"When did you first meet Claude?"

"You ask that question about anybody else I know—heh, heh, knew—and I'd draw a complete blank. Not Claude, though. October 14, 1917. You want the hour. It was three-thirty in the afternoon. I had just enlisted. My father had been busy pulling some strings to get me a commission, but I wanted to get in right away, and I had some idea that one should begin by serving in the ranks. I had just come out of the recruiting center downtown, quivering and shaking like a wet puppy, when this fellow on the way in stopped and stared at me. It was Claude, and I had never seen him before. He crouched next to the door and went 'wruf, wruf' at me. Then he stood up and offered me his hand. Do you remember how he used to say 'Ya-a-ale'?"

Morgan laughed.

"That's what he said as he came toward me. 'Ya-a-ale, brother. Eli, Eli, Ya-a-ale.' He had me mixed up with someone else. I'm Princeton. But we became friends for life."

Morgan laughed again, but his laughter was strained with politeness.

"We both ended up at the same camp in upstate New York, same unit as a matter of fact. You know, I've forgotten everything about it except that Claude and I were drunk for three days straight. We actually didn't stay much longer than those three days. His father and my father had the same idea. We both received our commissions on the same day. Claude went off to some southern camp and I went to Paris to join Pershing's staff as a very junior member . . ."

I lit a cigarette and glanced at the time. It was eight o'clock and I wondered when I'd see Elizabeth. My own activity and my boredom with the tape did not break the mood. It was as if I were present during the interview in a spirit state. As the conversation continued, small details of the room became clear. I discovered, for example, that the air-conditioning unit dripped and needed repair, that the day, though in the middle of the summer, was comfortable—therefore no need for the cooling unit. There was a liquor closet, complete with refrigerator, with a supply of Scotch, bourbon, rye, gin, and champagne. "The champagne is for special occasions." On one wall there was "An Excellent Photograph of the New York Skyline at Night." There are ghosts; I was one for almost an hour. As a listener, knowing of my own reality because of a glowing tip of a cigarette and my vague awareness of my physical being, I floated in and out of the room where the interview had taken place.

"Boo!" I exclaimed. Morgan and his friend did not hear me. They didn't know I was present. Weird emotion.

"Do you think that Claude's Blasingfield-Imperial deal was an unadulterated con game?" Morgan's tone was relaxed, almost careless. "Frankly, I never have. I realize that most people are apt to condemn him for it."

"God, I haven't heard anyone call it by that name since I last talked to Claude. How large a portion of your book deals with it?" He was obviously suspicious for the first time. This last sentence was measured, having none of the banter of the earlier recollection or the friendly get together. "How deeply are you going to dig into the Vanishing Indian?"

Then I remembered, if only in general terms. That was the era of the industrial pyramid. One company would hold the control of another, which in turn held control of still another, which in turn . . . And the primary purpose of each on the long string was to borrow money. The reason it was called the Vanishing Indian: the company that supported the inverted pyramid of borrowing companies was named Indian Oil and one day it vanished as a corporate entity. I never realized that Wester was responsible.

"I have to pay some attention to it," said Morgan. "Claude participated in its collapse and profited. He told me that he could implicate some ten others. He didn't mention your name."

"I'm glad of that." Either Morgan or the other man scraped his chair back and walked across the room. "What do you want to know about it?"

"As much as there is to know."

"Turn off the tape recorder."

"I have a good memory."

"I'd just as soon be in a position to deny everything."

"As you like."

Zip.

There was only an instant before the conversation continued.

Zip.

Raucous laughter from both men. "Oh yes, he was a damn fool. And so am I and all of us," the man said jubilantly. "You have that thing going again?"

"Just turned it on."

"When you think of the intrinsic value of money, I'm astonished at what I see done in its pursuit. Claude bought more legislators, bankers, and respectable newspaper editors than anyone I have ever known. And he did it without finesse. He would humiliate them. Those were the old days. It's not that way today."

"It's still being done."

"Perhaps it is. I don't see it."

I began to lose interest again. The two had a long philosophical discussion on the morality of Americans. I was surprised only that Morgan seemed determined to prove that his countrymen had deteriorated. He had seemingly forgotten the interview, preaching longer and longer without interruption from the other man. I began to doze.

Suddenly I was awake again.

"I will crucify that man for what he did to Claude!" It was Morgan speaking. The voice vibrated around me. It was whispered but magnified to a roaring presence. I shivered and was afraid to move in the dark. Morgan's words were malevolent. I felt as if I were being lapped by evil, that the voice breathed its venom on me. "He thinks he's safe, that I don't realize he created the Blasingfield-Imperial swindle. How dare he patronize Claude and belittle him into a puttee-wrapped army prankster! The man had no honor and has none still. I will skin off his self-righteous, pious cottoning and show him as the monster he was and still is."

Then I gasped. Morgan moaned and the gurgling wail slowy intensified to a series of hopeless bereaved sobs.

Elizabeth must have entered while I slept, for suddenly she was present. She snapped on the hall light. I turned sharply to see her, a dark figure, still wrapped in her black coat. She was staring at the tape recorder.

"You know a little more about Morgan than you ever knew before," she said tonelessly. "I loved him and tried to help him, but he hated me. I loved him all the more. He tried to stamp out all my love for him. We tortured one another as no two people have ever done before. Oh, God, I loved him."

She bit her lip and her eyes narrowed, squeezing together entirely. I thought she was going to cry. I rose from my seat and stepped toward her. She didn't cry. She finally composed herself, inhaling deeply. Her luminous eyes stared at me. "Would you mind if I asked you to leave?"

I shook my head, more in perplexity than to provide an answer.

"I need to be alone tonight. I'm very upset by that tape. I must think. Would you have breakfast with me in the morning? I'd like to see you in the morning."

I spent the night in the midtown YMCA. My exhaustion overcame me and I fell into a black dreamless sleep.

Five

I WOKE UP IN THE MORNING CRAMPED FROM THE NIGHT of having slept on a yielding mattress, sweaty from the steamy cubicle, struck by the thought that I was in a hell of a mess.

As I swung my legs to the floor, I recognized that Morgan Harper Stimmes would never have spent the night at the Y. And unaccountably I felt very sad. I wanted him alive again. Mornings are good times to think of him, for he had a sort of continuous morning vigor. I had only seen him once in the morning—I mean real morning, between dawn and lunch—and that was after a night of his being sleepless.

The bell had rung horribly, and I gasped from bed to dressing gown to door, pausing only to reach for a half-filled cigarette package, a booklet of matches, and a mouthful of rages against God and bell ringers.

I had opened the door and found Morgan, bright and cheerful, and a shallow-busted, hay-haired green pickle of a young girl wrapped on his arm.

"Look what I found," he said, as prideful as a man who had discovered a beach of gold dust. "I found her right here in New York." Awe at his discovery.

"You want coffee?" I asked, glancing at my watch and seeing that it was only five-thirty.

"Coffee?" He was stunned at my question. "Coffee when I have found the first two-dollar streetwalker since the war!"

She pulled her arm away. "Cut out the crap, Mac. Put up or shut up."

"Listen to her!" he shouted exultantly. "Have you heard anything like that since the war?"

I was speechless, and retreated. Morgan pushed the door open and began tugging his acquisition with him into the room.

"You're a madman," she said and pushed off his hand. Straightening out the cuff of her coat with a kind of shabby dignity, she continued, "I don't lie down with no madman, even if the price is right." She turned and stamped away, her high heels scraping across the hall floor, for even in haughtiness and anger she had a shuffling walk.

Morgan's face sagged. His eyelids crinkled with hurt. "Gertrude," he cried out. "Oh, my God, she's insulted."

"What did you expect?"

"Oh, my God, oh my God! Pour me a drink, Leeds. I'll be right back. Oh my God!" He dashed after her.

I watched him as he scrambled down the stairs, taking the many steps a stride at a time, until I could see him no longer and could only hear him—the heavy thud of his feet.

He caught up with her.

"My dear," I heard him say. Having already made a terrible mistake in his concept of that poor girl, he was blundering again by assuming the role of a man who was showing condescension.

"Don't give me any crap," she said.

His voice trailed low into a whisper, and all I could hear were the words "I'm sorry. God, am I sorry."

I closed the door to a crack. I was very amused by the scene I had just witnessed. My earlier feeling of belligerence at being wakened had dissipated. It had been a gray morning in the apartment when I first went to answer the bell. Now it was bright. Morning had come with Morgan. It was as good a way as any to begin a day, I decided. Then I laughed and went to make him a drink. I was almost in a mood to join him, but a sort of self-preserving wisdom overtook me, and I lit the stove under a pot of old coffee—I had a day before me and a job. Then I laughed some more, feeling giggly and awake.

I gave no thought to the underlying pins of Morgan's escapade. It was just another facet of his love for the anachronistic. A two-dollar streetwalker! Even in my amusement I realized that my reaction to the girl, had I been approached by her, would have been sorrow. That would have been typical of me. At that time I was saddened by the realization that I could not see beyond the frail girl and her unfortunate role.

Turning and seeing Morgan enter, I asked, "You had no intention of sleeping with her?"

"To be truthful," he said, "I didn't have one carnal thought." He spoke softly, distractedly. "That's what was wrong. I wasn't playing the game. It's my affliction. I have my own rules. If I could only believe in other people's."

I sensed that he was going to continue. He had his head turned toward the door through which he had just entered. Suddenly he seemed to realize that he had spoken more to himself than to me. His head snapped toward me. He smiled broadly. "What a hell of a thing to happen! I was puttering along Third Avenue, without a thought in the world other than that of finding a taxi."

"What were you doing on Third Avenue?" I handed him his drink.

"Leeds, you are distracting a perfectly fine story. What the hell would I be doing on Third Avenue. I was looking for a taxi!" He grinned and then swallowed deeply. "Ahh! That's how to get warm on a cold morning!"

"Is she gone?"

"Now you mean?"

"Now."

"Damn you, Leeds. I want to tell my story."

"Tell it, by all means. You don't mind if I drink my coffee?"

"You're an uncivilized son of a bitch!"

My coffee pot was perking violently, the brown scummy remains leaping from the spout. He was silent while I poured my coffee. I noticed that his face was pale. He had the look of a man practicing patience painfully. Our slight banter had annoyed him. He was staring at me quizzically.

"I'm sorry," I said. "I'll listen."

He still didn't speak.

"I'm listening." I turned to him, facing him. I was puzzled.

"You've set me up, haven't you? You've killed the amusement. Now I have to speak about myself and what I feel. This is damned lousy of you, Leeds. I want you to know that."

I didn't understand.

"It's arrogant of you," he continued. "It's not the first time since I've known you that I feel you're judging me."

"Cut it out, Morgan!" I put my cup down.

"What I did to that girl was unforgivable. You know it.

If I were the only one to know, I wouldn't feel so bad. I humiliated her, didn't I?" He was speaking rapidly of a sudden. "For the first time in my life I saw what I was doing through your eyes. It's damned uncomfortable. It's judgment, Leeds. You're judging me. Don't deny it."

"I don't know what you're talking about."

"The hell you don't!"

"The hell I do!"

Silence. For an interminable moment he studied me while sipping at his whiskey. The skin around his eyes crinkled into fine lines. His eyes were piercing. "You wouldn't have done that to her, would you?" he asked.

"I don't suppose I would."

"It would never have occurred to you to find it strange that prostitution still existed at the two-dollar rate."

"I think I would have felt sorry for her."

"You're ruining my life," he said quietly, again as if to himself. "Goddamn it!" he exploded. "Hasn't it occurred to you that each of us has a course of life to run and we only confuse it if we go around feeling sorry for our fellows. It doesn't help ours, and it doesn't help theirs."

"Tell me about her, for Christ sakes! That's all you want to do, isn't it?"

"You're an insufferable son of a bitch."

"Of course I am. I'm a friend of yours."

He finally laughed. He finished his drink and thrust the empty glass at me.

"More?" I asked.

"You bet your sweet life, more."

It was time for me to smile. While I refilled his glass, he began his story.

"I was leaning against a building in great weariness when she approached. I wasn't aware of her being there at first. I had just yelled my lungs out at a taxi, which ignored me, and I was manufacturing cuss words to suit the occasion. You listening?"

"I'm just getting you some ice."

"You bastard, I'm beyond ice and you know it."

"No ice, then." I handed him his warm drink.

"You saw her. She's a shadow of a person. There's no courage to her bearing. When she speaks, her voice is a kind of harsh angry whimper. 'I had a bad night, mister,' she says. 'You interested?' Interested in her bad night? 'Not a bit,' I said, startled by her presence but quick to know my answer to a question such as that. 'You know what I'm talkin' about?' she asks."

He closed his eyes for a moment. I waited. When he opened his eyes, they were glistening.

" 'You know what means to get laid?' she asks. The poor consumptive little dear had her eyes cast down as if she were embarrassed. 'I've just laid a young woman,' I said. 'Then you ain't interested in laying me,' she said. She not once looked me in the eye. I felt as if I were participating in some shadow play. She began to move away. 'Is that an invitation, young lady?' I asked. She looked up at me. I'm not sure she understands what invitation means. 'You might as well know it, mister, I'm a two-buck whore and I'm in business. You either want it or you don't. Anything fancy will cost you more.' " He laughed. "When I asked her for a definition of 'fancy,' she was most crudely explicit, and she had a price list to go with the event. The only times she did not avert her eyes was when she mentioned price. As you can well imagine, this meeting was beginning to fascinate me. And to make matters even more to my liking, one of those old junk wagons came down the cobblestones at that moment. Its ancient nag, starved to the ribs, clip clopping. And then I remembered the sounds of my twenties, the wonderful years of milk wagons and yawning simple women. My God! I thought. A two-dollar prostitute! I must show her to Leeds."

He had circled around me and away from me. He was now staring out of my dirty window, watching the El tracks. "Do you understand?" he asked in a whisper.

How many years ago was that? I couldn't remember. Or, at least, I didn't try to remember. It had been a vivid moment, but only vivid now because of what I had learned about Morgan. Had he died in some splashy heroic incident, I would never have remembered his pathetic "Do you understand?" But, of course, there was no longer room in our world for the splashy or the heroic. I think most of us today would be amused by efforts of heroism. They are anachronisms, unfitted to our mood.

By the time I reached the street I had lost my early morning droop of sleepiness. The crisp air was revival and I was bursting with hallelujah. In the swingtime of a half-hour I had lurched from sad memory to a feeling of vitality at a new day.

It was eight-thirty before I saw Elizabeth. I walked all the way to the Village, stopping only briefly at a drugstore for a doughnut and a cup of coffee. (I don't know of any city or town more wide awake at eight-thirty in the morning than New York.)

She was more alert than I expected. In fact, I was surprised by her. She still had her mourning look, the tinge of sorrow—black dress. But her eyes were bright, anticipating, and there was a touch of color to her lips.

"I expected you earlier," she said.

She took me by the arm, leading me into the apartment.

I felt awkward having her touch me.

"I hope you haven't had breakfast," she continued. "I've been waiting until you arrived. I thought it would be a gay way to begin the day. It was so depressing when we parted."

"I had . . . c-c-coffee . . ." I stammered.

She laughed before I finished the rest of my sentence. "Hardly enough for a man in the morning." She tugged me after her into the kitchen. The table had been set. There was a tablecloth with a floral design. Shining silver at each place. Plates. "Morgan always told me that you had no appreciation for food or women."

"He was right about the food." I recovered a little from my surprise.

She turned her head slightly and stared at my eyes. She winked. "We'll see," she said.

The domestic life has its virtues. Of that I'm certain. However, it must have been the creation of women in an attempt to schedule existence, to order the lives of errant males.

Breakfast consisted of the setting up of a schedule. Though she said, "It's delightful to have you here with me," her delight was in arranging me and my time so that my presence was only peripheral to her own movements. Breakfast, though pleasant—most superficially pleasant—and full of chitchat, left me hungry for the meat of meaningful language. There was a suggestiveness in her manner, casual glances with passionate undertones, but nothing more. It was "Do you like jam on your toast? I find men can't stand toast without jam."

It was maddening. I felt the constraint of the recent death and the knowledge that I was breakfasting with a "widow." I place quotations around "widow" only because it needs some conditional mark, because it creates an emotion, a softness of voice, a politeness, a sufferance.

I retreated into "her" schedule of "my" life gladly, not knowing how to make my own pattern.

It was with a deep sense of relief that I moved to the study. There was in my mind a willingness—an eagerness—to retire to Morgan's material. Somewhere within it was a name of a lawyer, some explanation of what Morgan intended me to do. But first I had to wait until she stacked the dishes. As I sat down and ripped open a carton—under the watchfulness of Elizabeth, who sat on a hard chair in the corner—the envelope I saw first had the scrawl *Autograph* on its front.

The word carried me back.

It was approximately two in the afternoon. (I give the time only to explain that there was a reason for being at a stand with a glass of watery orange juice and a hot dog in my hands, grabbing at lunch.)

Suddenly a pair of hands ripped both juice and dog from my hands and put them on the counter.

"What in hell?" I exploded. Then I saw Morgan's face with a disapproving look. He grinned, then laughed.

"This is the shock of my life," he said. "You have fallen into the pit of modern horrors. Come along, Leeds, and have lunch with me."

I grinned sheepishly. "I have to make a living, Morgan," I protested.

"Foolishness!" he exploded, and moved me—my elbow as his rudder—into a waiting taxi.

"Hey, I didn't pay the man!"

"Let that be his punishment for serving such garbage." He turned a moment toward the stand, facing the shocked counterman. "Fie! Fie on you!" Morgan shouted. Then he threw back his head and roared delightedly at what he had said. He flipped a half-dollar dexterously at the man, and we were in the cab.

I was speechless. Morgan continued his abuse of lunch counters. The cabbie was about to make a comment, and turned his head, his lips ready for at least one word. Then I could see his lips form the expression What the hell, and he turned back to his driving.

My noting this betrays me. I was in some measure dulled by Morgan's carping with the modern world's minor or backwash abrasions. He didn't really mean to pick apart the details of the world he didn't like. He did it to jar me from my compliant acceptance, but I was bored instead.

"You're beyond redemption," he said when we had arrived at a shabby bar deep on the West Side. "If only you would listen." Then abruptly, explaining the bar, "You will order lamb chops and vin rouge. The cook and the bartender are from Marseilles. Only sailors come here. Imagine, in New York, a genuine café with food that will surprise you."

From that moment on the only thing that surprised me was Morgan. I hardly remember the food or the wine. It came and went.

"I thought it might interest you to know that I have a son," he said. "I have just spent an hour with him and saw his mother. And perhaps it might confound you: this is the first time I have ever laid eyes on him. If I'm banal in any of my comments, forgive me, for I don't really understand the impact of actually having a son." He leaned with his elbows on the table, his eyebrows thatched in puzzlement, his eyes staring.

"You knew you had a son before today?"

"When I returned from Egypt, I went to tell a woman that her husband—a friend of mine—had died gloriously. To be truthful, I had no way of knowing how he died. She invited me in, mixed me a martini, and then as if there was nothing else to do, we went to bed together. I felt very little emotion. She was satisfying a deep need.

"The necessary number of months went by and she wrote me that we—mind you, we—had a baby boy. She said it was a very good child and was comely. And then she wrote the words 'Thank you.' I was stunned, of course, and I waited. Nothing more ever came from her. I heard once that she had married a screenwriter some years later."

Morgan slapped his hands together as though still pondering. "And that was all until a phone call this morning. It was a simple message. Oh, dear God, make me repeat it right! She said, 'I think it's time you met your son. He has always known that you are his father. He's quite nice.' "

Morgan slumped back in his seat. "What in God's name possessed that woman to tell a child that he was a bastard! She's mad, utterly mad!"

"How was the meeting?"

Morgan tried to smile but bafflement and the memory of his morning erased the lift of his lips. "How can I tell you? Step by step would make us both cry. We met at

Pennsylvania Station. She said she had some errands to do. She left the boy and me together. We talked about nothing—How's school? Fine. Where are you going to school? Choate. That's a good school. Nothing but inane pass-the-time questions and answers. He was an attractive kid."

Morgan stopped to study the flyspecked ceiling and then the half glass of wine in front of him. Then he drank it quickly and poured it full again from the bottle.

"There wasn't anything else?"

"There was one more thing. He asked me for my autograph."

"What does that mean?" Elizabeth asked.

"Probably your father's signature," I said casually, hopeful that I sounded casual, and tossed the envelope aside. Though repetitive, I again use the word casual. I suspected my explanation was right, but Morgan was keen enough in his use of symbols and code to have used *Autograph* as a private key for me.

Elizabeth may not have understood the code but she understood casual gestures for what they are, or perhaps what they might be—designed efforts at concealments. I should have known better.

"May I see it, please?" she asked.

I hoped my explanation was correct. In any case, I had to react swiftly. I threw her the envelope and dug deeply into the carton for a tape. "Want to hear a tape?" I asked in return.

"Oh yes," she said and tossed the envelope back into the carton as she reached for the tape. It was too easy, I thought.

"You have the recorder set up?" I asked.

"All set," she said exultantly.

"You thread the tape and I'll glance through the rest of the box."

She hesitated, a vague suspicion clouding her face.

"I'm not going to steal anything," I said.

She smiled and left with the tape. I quickly put the envelope she had discarded into my inside coat pocket. It was a ridiculous victory, because I didn't know whether it was or was not a victory. However, it gave me pleasure of the most intense sort.

I scrambled through the box, noting the orderly process of filing the research material in neat folders. Each folder seemed to contain a different interview. It then occurred to me that he had the tapes translated into typescript. I might lose the mood and the emotional context of the tape, but I'd have the facts. While I stared at the files, I decided that I had to have them removed. I would never accomplish anything under the gaze of Elizabeth.

"Ken, Ken," she suddenly shouted happily. "Come listen, he recorded my voice when I was a child. Quick! Quick!"

She was delightful. As the voice of a little girl spoke hesitantly, obviously aware that her voice was being recorded, she was dancing in the middle of the living room. All artificiality had disappeared. Her happiness was completely spontaneous. Listening to the voice, I could suddenly see her as Morgan first saw her. I could see the child that became the woman. I could see the child because at that moment she was that child.

She grabbed my hand and spun me with her. Awkwardly I tried to keep up with her. Suddenly she stopped and looked down at my feet. "I wish you weren't lame," she said. "I can't stand your being lame!" Her last sentence was almost a scream. Then she was quiet and stared at my face. Shame was on her face.

It was strange. For several minutes neither of us spoke a word. I half listened to her voice on the tape, a young girl speaking carefully, self-consciously. "My lessons are complete. I have completed them earlier so that I might attend this party tonight and be Daddy's hostess. Even though I am very young, I am very accomplished in helping Daddy . . ."

She half closed her eyes and hugged me, clinging to me as though in fear. "Take me," she whispered. "I'm so very alone. I need you." She gripped me. "Now!"

Six

IT WAS AN ODD BARGAIN. DURING THAT WEEKEND I WAS the male praying mantis, offering myself to be devoured by the female and then being devoured. However, I traded each hour, each encounter, for Morgan's records and boxes containing the research for his book. And it wasn't my choice. Almost as if she had measured her need in terms of the records, she used them to humiliate me. In my innocence I wanted nothing but Elizabeth. My own sensuality was almost totally brutalized.

There was a terrible symbolism to bear with each act of sex. A crate or a file was moved from the study to the door. Aroused by hidden fire, she rose from the bed in pale nudity, a grim glare on her face; then I could hear her moving one of the files to the front door.

I followed her the first few times and asked if I could help. I suppose I was smiling, for I know I was amused by the sight of her—the quivering naked shanks, the tiny bended body—pushing cartons along the floor.

She stood up straight and glared at me defiantly, her tiny breasts rigid—strangely angry-appearing—and then bent down again and continued to shove. I didn't bother to offer aid after those experiences. All feelings of the sensual were lessened after them. I even began to dread the sound of her moving Morgan's research.

Even as I left at six Monday morning, she stood a few feet from me as I moved the research into the hallway from the apartment. Her arms were akimbo, her face showing no emotion. "In return," she said, "for the envelope in your coat pocket that you stole earlier—Autograph, remember!—I expect you back during the evening next Friday. Everything you want is in that envelope." Then she snickered and disappeared into the bedroom. I could hear her hurl herself on the bed in a jubilant leap.

I closed the door.

I knew then that she had gone through every scrap of Morgan's research.

What was in the envelope? It was a note from Morgan to me. There was indeed everything I wanted in it. There was no typical Morgan language, nothing more than a list of names, positions, and addresses.

There was nothing for me to do but go to work—work even with the niggling or perhaps not so niggling doubts of Elizabeth's motives.

The lawyer flew in from Washington. I was surprised that Morgan had chosen a lawyer at that distance, and when I spoke to him on the phone, I was even more surprised. He had the voice of a small peeping bird, strangely childlike.

We met in a cocktail lounge at Kennedy. He wanted only to talk briefly and get acquainted and then fly back to Washington.

He seemed to have no difficulty in knowing who I was. He strode right to me. A ponderous man, with a bulbish avocado head, a balloon of a belly balanced on two spindly legs, and an innocent "I-am-prepared-to-accept-anything-you-tell-me" face, he soon taught me that looks are indeed deceiving. The voice was entirely out of character. However, I became accustomed to it surprisingly soon.

"Mr. Leeds!" He clapped a heavy hand on my shoulder. "Morgan often startles me with his accuracy of description." He laughed. "At least, I've learned to trust his descriptions." His name was Herman Touse. "You pronounce it 'twos.' They went aboard the ark by twos." I rose to greet him, but he pressed me back to my seat at the bar and sat down at the next stool. "I think we should get down to business. It's really quite simple, even if it seems complicated at times. Human beings make things complicated."

"I'm willing to grant that," I said, smiling.

"However," he said, "I must first deal with a human complication."

"Elizabeth, I bet."

His eyes snapped at me. Just for a second I felt he knew everything about Elizabeth, and possibly a great deal about me. "Elizabeth," he concurred. "A very lovely young lady, a very seductive one. I've seen her, fortunately without her seeing me. A stunning creature."

"I know her well enough to realize that she's a problem."

His eyes narrowed. "I'm sure you do."

"If we're going to be all business, maybe you can answer me one thing—I just don't understand how she got all the records."

"Very understandable request." He smiled slightly. "I sent them to her."

The bartender arrived at that moment. Before I could register my surprise or ask a question, we were involved in the routine of a bartender earning his living. My surprise probably registered in another way: I ordered a double Scotch, finishing the single one I already had. And I waited a moment, during the wait after ordering, to ask, "Why?"

Touse smiled grimly and did not say anything in reply until the drinks came, the bar was mopped, and the bartender moved back to his neutral faraway corner.

"I'll have to answer candidly. It was for a simple reason." Quickly a fleeting smile. "Do you want that reason?"

"You're stalling," I said.

"How very quick of you! Yes, I am. I'm evaluating you. That's arrogance, and I don't think you deserve arrogance. I delivered the cartons, or, rather, I had them delivered—first cataloguing everything—because I was told to." He sipped gingerly at his drink. He seemed to think that the subject was closed. "I received the copy of the letter that Morgan sent to you about Elizabeth. A very meticulous man. He kept copies of everything. I think that has something to do with ego."

"Still stalling."

His eyes flickered over my face, as if he were making a quick analysis of me, as if my feelings could be seen.

"Morgan instructed me to send the material. The request didn't come from Mrs. Stimmes. Does that seem surprising?"

"Surprising? No. It's strange that he gave them to you and then had them returned to Elizabeth."

"It surprised me." He studied me again. "It's my practice to try to know those I work for and with. At the moment, that means you and Mrs. Stimmes."

"Know enough?"

"Frankly, I'm confused. Elizabeth Stimmes is my problem. I accept you. However, I did not expect her to give you my name. She did, didn't she?"

"She permitted me to have it."

"That's an odd way of putting it."

"It was an odd permission."

He looked thoughtful. "It doesn't matter if it was odd. She let you have it. I just didn't expect it."

"I gather you were going to get in touch with me eventually."

"In one more week. Time is a relative judgment. I believed that one more week would provide a sufficient time for Mrs. Stimmes to give you my name. I must say that there was an element of surprise in your timing. Morgan forecast it within two days."

"Did Morgan fire you?" It was a good time for bluntness.

"Yes and no." He chortled. "He fired me, but I was insistent on continuing. I was too interested. Finally he agreed to have me continue."

Suddenly I was aware that I had finished my drink. I glanced at his glass. Though it was impossible to express my feeling at his answer, I knew I was sinking deeper into a sticky pool. "You're not drinking," I said as I motioned to the bartender.

"And you're not normally a drinker," he said. "I will do my best to serve your interests because they are Morgan's interests by intention. However, I suggest you be careful of drinking." He smiled fleetingly. "With anyone, including me in the future. You may as well understand that I will sacrifice you whenever your interests are in conflict with Morgan's intentions."

I would remember that statement later as a basis of judging his behavior. "What were Morgan's intentions?" I received another drink, accepting it with some internal sheepishness.

"As I said, I have a copy of the letter he wrote you. I also know generally of conversations he has held with you. I have some few instructions from Morgan that I must hold as privileged. These few things should not in any way cause any difficulty for you." His brow furrowed. "Were you in any way involved in the arrangements for disposing of Morgan's body?" he asked.

"Not at all. I assumed you made them."

"I made none of them. Consequently, I have ghoulishly had the movement of the body under observation. For your information, Morgan's remains are now in an urn. I still don't understand the arrangements, because the individuals involved don't understand them."

"Elizabeth," I suggested.

"She seems to be as mystified by them. It was, as a matter of fact, her curiosity that prompted me to become curious." He still seemed puzzled. "Morgan changed in the past weeks. I had only known him for a few months, but I was intrigued by his confusions with our modern society. His letter to you was one of the most extraordinary documents I have ever read." His eyes turned toward me as if asking my confirmation.

"I agree," I said.

He glanced at his watch. "I have to catch my plane. This was a great pleasure, Mr. Leeds. I am going to give you my card. I'm only an hour away. And having an office in New York, I'm here quite often, in any case." He stood up and handed me a card. He shook my hand. After I glanced down at the card and looked up again, I discovered he had gone. I wasn't certain that anything had been accomplished, but I had a very secure feeling that I was no longer foundering, that Morgan's intentions were real, that uneasiness had vanished. If another replaced it, I couldn't yet define it.

That evening, after returning to my apartment, the phone rang. I looked at my watch in a sort of appraisal of probabilities of who might be calling. It was nine-thirty. I thought it might be Elizabeth.

"Hello."

"This is George Teagarten."

"Yes." The name meant nothing to me.

"Brenther's."

I then remembered my conversation with Boyd Hall at the publisher's and his telephone conversation with his boss. "I know," I said. "Boyd told me to write you a letter about Morgan's book."

"Good," he said crisply. "I don't think a letter is necessary. I'd like to discuss it with you."

"I haven't talked to the people at *View* yet."

"That's not essential."

"I have to teach some classes during the day. But under some circumstances . . ."

He didn't let me finish. "If you're free tonight, I'd just as soon thrash it around this evening."

"It's nine-thirty."

"Too late for you?"

"No. I'm just somewhat curious. The other day I gathered I was going to have a problem to see you. Now you call me during the evening and suggest we meet the same night. Wouldn't that make you curious?"

He laughed; I sensed that his laughter was forced, for it sounded artificial. "I suppose you're entitled to an explanation." I rankled at the word *suppose*. "I've given the book some thought. I want to discuss it."

The arrogant son of a bitch, I thought. "Where do you want to meet?"

"I'm in Connecticut, at home," he said. "I'm probably not too far away from you. I'll come to your house, if you like."

"You come here," I said. "It's not a house, it's an apartment and a small one at that."

"Fine," he said.

I gave him the address, and he said he'd arrive around ten. He seemed to have no awareness that my mood and tone were petulant. I had a distinct feeling, also, that I was in the superior position. And I credited this position to some maneuver performed by Touse.

I looked around the apartment. Rather neat, I thought, except for Morgan's cartons, which were piled sloppily between the desk and the closet kitchen. While not one of those meticulous bachelors, I felt enough pride to be somewhat neat, especially knowing a stranger was about to judge me and could do it by judging my apartment. I rose and straightened out the cartons. When I finished, they were neatly on top of one another.

George Teagarten turned out to be a young man roofed with unruly red hair, appearing to be even younger than I. When he first entered my apartment, his moonish ruddy face scanned the contents of the room like a moving spotlight. When his eyes fell on my pile of Morgan's research, they seemed to soften. I suddenly knew that his agreement to come to see me had a basic motive: he wanted to know if I had the material.

"Glad we could get to talk this evening," he said enthusiastically.

"I'm interested in what we're going to talk about."

"I want to talk about the book," he said pleasantly, his right hand gesturing toward the pile.

"Surprised that I have Morgan's material?"

"Lord, you are suspicious of me!" Open-faced innocence.

"Would you like a drink?"

"Agreeable."

"Anything special?"

"Anything."

I started to make him a drink, and throwing Touse's caution to the wind, also fixed myself one. His eyes kept straying back to the pile.

"Have you gone through the material?" he asked.

"Some of it. I really wasn't going to write you until I knew what was in it."

"What's your opinion of what you've seen?"

"I can't give you one. I don't have one yet."

"Hell, Ken," he said, "you must have some idea if it is as explosive as I've been led to believe."

I recognized the easy familiarity as a device to relax my hostility. "George," I countered, "I don't know what you've been led to believe. Morgan never discussed the book with me." I dropped two ice cubes into a brimming glass of bourbon and handed it to him. My own drink was much more conservative in quantity and much better in quality.

"You're determined not to take any crap from me, aren't you?"

"I just have a feeling that something else, other than Morgan's book, is behind your questions, behind your interest. It's a pretty strong feeling."

"Well, that's candid!"

"Expressions of that sort don't help me much. If you want to know what I think: I think you use that kind of remark as an evasion to a direct question, or an implied question."

He plopped down on my one soft chair and ducked behind his glass. Then he swallowed a full third of his drink. "You're a real cool cookie!" He recognized that he had again done what I had accused him of and laughed suddenly. "Hell! You're right, of course. But that doesn't improve things, does it?"

"No."

And he laughed again. "I'll come clean," he said. "I don't have anything else left. You've taken away my bag of tricks."

"Am I right?" I asked.

"Something else on my mind? You betcha." He gulped at his drink again. "In case you don't know it, my company is publicly owned. In other words, I have a crowd of people who own my company. However, there are a couple of large owners."

"Two."

"Actually more than two. But two is the correct figure when you add up the number of my shareholders who are concerned—did I say concerned?—I meant worried about the Stimmes book."

I relaxed in the presence of a young man who was now obviously telling the truth.

"You have a tape recorder?" he asked.

"Yes."

"I'd like to play a small piece of tape that the two received in the mail, received without explanation."

While I located the recorder and connected it, Teagarten helped himself to another drink, pouring from a bottle of my better bourbon. He was most efficient in finding the ice. He offered to replenish my drink. "Still have some," I mumbled. He grinned.

Then he threw me a small spool. "That's one of them." I threaded the tape. "Not much on it," he explained, "but it's spooky."

I began the machine and heard nothing but the hum.

"Be patient," he said. He drank. His face was now grave.

And then the voice came. "I will crucify that man for what he did to Claude!" That was all there was.

"Morgan Harper Stimmes," Teagarten said. "Unmistakably Morgan Harper Stimmes."

"Two men received that tape?" I asked.

"Two I know of."

"It was taken out of a much longer tape. He was only referring to one man."

"Did you send it?"

I laughed. "You don't ask that question seriously?"

"Who the hell did, then?"

I immediately guessed that it was Elizabeth. But I didn't think it was a necessary part of this evening to make guesses. "I don't have the vaguest idea, unless it was Morgan himself."

"That, damn it, is the same thought that one of the two had. That's why I called it spooky."

"Morgan's dead."

"That doesn't mean that he didn't arrange for the tapes to be sent now."

"What does this mean about the book's publication?"

"Of course we'll publish it."

"Let me guess: You want to make sure it doesn't crucify anyone."

"We have an obligation to meet the terms of the contract," he said.

I smiled. "The terms of the contract ended when Morgan died," I said.

"You did send the tapes," he said accusingly.

"As a matter of fact, I didn't, and I don't know who did. I just recognize the strength of a new position. Blame me?"

"You may as well know that you're not dealing with me. You're bucking two powerful guys. They can kill publication completely, if they want."

"I don't think that will be necessary."

He grinned again. "I didn't think it would be. Actually, I think it might be a fine book full of nostalgia, a kinda interesting story of one of America's tycoons. High living. That kinda thing."

"I agree."

"Can we whittle it out tonight?"

"Sorry. I can't. You'll have to check with Herman Touse. Also, I have to find a writer to finish Morgan's book."

"Why don't you do it?"

"No, thanks. I've got a job I'm happy with."

"Who's Herman Touse?"

"A lawyer."

"Oh, that Touse." He appeared to be thoughtful. "I wouldn't put it past Touse to have mailed those tapes."

"Just met the gentleman."

"Believe me, he's capable."

"Did you know Morgan?" I said.

"I've talked to him several times. I can't say that I knew him." His eyes moved back to me. "Tell me the truth, Ken. You don't really understand what's going on, either."

"Truthfully, I'm just following orders left me by Morgan. Do I have to understand it?"

"No curiosity?"

"Plenty of it. I don't feel any compulsion to do anything but what I was told to do." I was lying, but I didn't think it was particularly his business.

"You haven't talked to the *View* people?"

"Not yet."

"Good. I'm going to recommend three writers for the book. *View* will probably go along."

"What makes you so sure *View* will want to continue Morgan's deal?"

"My men also own a substantial amount of their shares. I told you they could kill publication. They want a nice quiet nostalgic piece about a tycoon. Period. They have a certain amount of vanity. They'd like to be in the book on those terms." He grinned, flashing his teeth. "No question of publication, just the kind of publication."

"And I'm no muckraker."

"Whether it's justified or not, my two men have a lot of respect for you. They think you sent the tapes. They respect that kinda move."

"It's something Claude Wester might have done."

"That's exactly what one of them said."

"Very funny," I said. I was thinking that the comment was almost true. I was certain that Claude Wester's daughter had done the sending.

"Funny," he agreed.

Seven

I DIDN'T FEEL SLEEPY THAT NIGHT. TEAGARTEN'S VISIT was probably responsible. I decided it was time for me to know the material that Morgan had put together.

Thus, I squatted down next to the cartons and dug in. For once I was going to avoid the tapes and begin reading the notes. I was also curious to discover if Morgan had begun to formulate some system, some point of view, in which to pour the facts of Claude Wester's life.

Despite my well-intended design, I almost immediately found myself staring at the cartons and thinking about Elizabeth. What was she doing? I wondered. Why had she sent the edited tapes? I wasn't naïve about her, even if I was again finding a lurking sensation deep within myself that was labeled with her name and the memory of her body. I knew she was capable of almost anything.

Only one conclusion made sense to me: she was about to blackmail her father's former associates. She was not in the least concerned that the profits from the magazine piece or the book would go to Morgan's bastard son.

Finally I broke out of my daydream and began to read. I skipped those notes that dealt primarily with Claude Wester and his business manipulations. (Morgan would never forgive me for using "manipulations.") He and they bored me. I wondered if I could ever convince a writer to undertake the book; I couldn't convince myself that it was worthwhile or necessary.

I sped through the material, picking up small details of the lives of the rich during the twenties. Such as: "Edgerton noted that Claude owned a house on Fifth that he called his Influence Manor. Used it for entertaining. Loaned it to politicians as base for New York visits. With it, also loaned hot blondes. When unoccupied, Claude filled its ballroom with musicians. He would sit alone in the rear on a straight chair. Drinking brandy from a tumbler, he would listen to whatever they wanted to play, never making a comment. Finally, the evening would end when Claude pitched over drunk, spilling the remains of the bottle on the oak floor. The musicians would tiptoe out, leaving him sprawled there. Sometimes the group came from Harlem. Sometimes it was a string quartet. Once it was a full orchestra."

Morgan didn't comment or explore this anecdote. It was just a brief portrait of a wealthy self-indulgent man with a singular method of lonely drinking. I thought it was hardly the sort of portrait that Morgan would accept.

I was struck by the lack of Morgan's appraisal of the interviewees and the stories. His touch was missing in all the material I read. There was nothing of him in any of the notes. I had never seen the type of research that he used to write from. It was possible that he laid it out in this colorless blank fashion and then expanded during the writing. I became intrigued by the plethora of similar stories, wondering how Morgan adjusted his hero worship of Wester with the evidence he was compiling that was directly contrary.

I was surprised when I turned one sheet over to see that Morgan had lightly penciled several sentences on the back of the page.

Though it was difficult to decipher, I decided that it said: "Dear Lord, I'm tired of all this. I wish I were dead. This is Hell."

I smiled. I sympathized. Had Morgan emphasized this thought with a heavy pencil or used some mark of punctuation, I might have given it more importance, but the material was having the same effect on me.

Then I remembered.

Morgan had rented a house in Brewster on Cape Cod. He had somehow talked *View Magazine* into underwriting a story on the—quote—tragic desolate landscape and peoplescape of a summer colony after the summer people have left—unquote—and *View* was footing the bill for two weeks in October.

On a Friday morning I received a postcard from him, saying: "Dear *Lord,* I'm *tired* of all this. This is *Hell.* Come quick and spend weekend. Have much whiskey and am lonely as hell."

The underlined Lord, tired, and Hell were emphatic enough, and I had no other plans. So I left that evening, driving up slowly, stopping for dinner near Hartford, wondering how I'd find him in the middle of the night. I wasn't even sure I'd find Brewster. I didn't, stopping instead around ten at a motel.

The following morning I found him sitting in a deck chair on the beach below the house. It was one of those moody fall days, the sky gloomy with black-etched clouds. It was cold.

Morgan had covered himself with a thick Indian blanket, looping its edge over his head. He was staring morosely out at the mud of the flats. Brewster is on the Cape Bay and the ocean tide goes out for over a mile.

He was apparently aware that I was there even though he showed no awareness. I had a feeling that I shouldn't intrude, so I simply stood there for several minutes within his sight but to the far left.

He finally said, "This was a lousy idea, Leeds. There's no fun in it. Hell, there's no people."

"I saw people," I said.

"I mean pee-pul. No one left misses the summer people. The ones you saw don't seem to realize that they've lost anything. They're living as if the summer never happened. I probably picked a bad area. There must be sadness somewhere about the summer being over."

"Are you supposed to take photographs?"

"I took them."

"Won't they tell the story of tragic desolation?"

He turned his head for the first time and glared at me. "Pictures," he said contemptuously, "never tell a story when I'm writing it. Words are the poetry of emotion."

"Amen," I replied with a smile.

"Damn it, Leeds, you're a bastard. Let's go have a drink. It's cold out here."

It was a small house, obviously not prepared for any autumn or winter tenant. The brisk wind made a howling sound as it slipped through the thin summer skin of the gray boards. He had not bothered to make the house very habitable, having pushed back a few dust covers so that he might sit on the furniture. There was an empty whiskey bottle in the middle of the floor of the living room.

Glancing out the front window out to the flats, I understood a little about Morgan's emotions. To a man of enthusiasms, the bleak vistas had nothing to offer; the food on which enthusiasm lives was missing. There was nothing gay. There was only a scene a nature lover might enjoy. It occurred to me that he should never have considered doing a story on the desolation, tragic or otherwise, of the winter life of anything. He was a summer person.

I went into the kitchen, where he was fumbling with a newly opened bottle of Scotch. His hands were shaking.

"This kind of story is not your cup of tea," I commented.

"Christ, it's cold," he said, refusing to be drawn into any discussion.

"It's not a steam-heated apartment."

"Very perceptive of you." No smile on his face. He opened the refrigerator and dug into a bag of ice. Other than the ice, there was nothing else inside.

"No food?" I commented.

"What do I need food for? I can't and don't cook."

"Where do you eat?"

"There's a couple of lesbians renting a cottage in the next town. One of them is a fine cook."

I laughed. "How did you manage to make an arrangement like that?"

"I asked the man in the store where I could find a nearby restaurant, and one of the young ladies was standing there. They're outcasts in this winter world." He held up the two glasses and stared at them. "I hope you've had breakfast. Lunch isn't until two today. They're going walking on the flats."

We didn't speak again until we had both seated ourselves in the living room.

"It is just possible that you're right," he finally said.

"Are you talking about what I'm thinking or about something I said." I was thinking that his description of the two girls as outcasts was also appropriate to his own state.

"Probably both," he said. He smiled. "You often stick with the same thought longer than you should. This story is not my cup of tea."

"It doesn't fit you. I suspect it wasn't your idea to begin with."

"You're wrong. It was my idea." He had already finished his drink and was pouring himself another from the bottle he had placed between his feet. "I made a mistake in my analysis of people. Most summer people make the same mistake. They think they'll be missed after they're gone."

"I'm sure that the money they spend is missed."

His eyebrows arched in puzzlement. "You live in a mechanical world, Leeds. You never think of the romance of anything. Regardless of your being right, there's no fun in the way you think. The winter people should feel sad. Instead they go about their business, ignoring the change of season. They should savor the events of the past summer and dream of the joys of the next."

"What are you going to write?"

"I don't know. I could do a piece on the way it really is, but it would take the heart out of me. To write it would destroy my own dream of the way it ought to be and the way every summer person thinks it is."

On that note, that particular line of conversation ended. I was dismayed at the despair he was showing, so I was pleased that he abruptly began to ask about mutual friends in New York. Though he had been gone only a week, he talked as though years had intervened between this moment and the last time he had been in the city.

He had an amazing capacity for drinking without showing effects. However, I had very little ability to hold my liquor. As I was loudly holding forth on the sins of a friend who had once stabbed his wife in a buttock, the front door opened and two women entered the house. They glowered at the room, as if it were hostile ground to be taken by dint of arms, and then at me.

There was an odd similarity about the two, although in appearance they were strikingly different. One was plump, breastless, and severe-faced. The other was softly slim, well formed, and even-featured. They both had quick darting eyes and grim tight mouths.

Morgan stood up quickly. I staggered to my feet.

"Beachcombing all over?" he asked.

They didn't answer. The thin one glanced at the other, as though for assurance.

A flicker of a smile crossing his lips, Morgan said, "Allow me to introduce a new guest to your dining table—Ken Leeds." Then turning toward me, a hand gracefully dipping at each, "And this is Viola Grafton and Miss Martha Kempton." Viola was the chubby one.

I mumbled my pleasure at meeting them.

"Is this the one you told us about, Morgan?" Viola asked drily.

"Viola," said Martha, not giving him a chance to reply, "he makes me feel very uneasy. He's very ugly. Quite disgusting. We won't serve dinner to him. Doesn't he make you uneasy, Viola?"

"Yes, sweetie, me, too." And the two of them left as abruptly as they entered.

I had blunted and confused emotions. I should have understood that no one could have said what she had said without being prompted. The words were too cutting and too cruel to be casual.

Morgan's smile broadened. After the door slammed shut, he fell back into his chair in helpless laughter. Through peals, he managed to say, "You . . . should . . . see . . . the . . . expression . . . on . . . your . . . face!"

Still standing, wavering unsteadily, I stared down at him. "For Christ sakes, stop laughing!" I demanded.

For the next hour my confusion continued. We didn't refer to the girls, but conversation would bite into subjects of food, and he would begin giggling. "Can you cook, Leeds?" he'd ask and then roar on, unable to speak coherently.

We finally went out to find a restaurant or a diner.

"I know of a place," he said. We left the main road and wound down a dismal tar road for several miles. He now had the hiccoughs along with his sudden burbles of laughter.

"This doesn't look promising," I offered.

The dead beach loomed ahead, gray dunes rolling down to the flats. He stopped the car at an uninviting shack. A wisp of dirty smoke coiled from a smudgy pipe in the roof.

I suddenly understood the laughter. Somewhere in his expansive nature there was a serpent; it had struck and I was the victim.

"Not very funny," I said. I think I felt more betrayed by my own judgment than merely shocked. "You bastard son of a bitch!"

"It was just a joke," he said. His smile was fading. He hiccoughed.

"I'm going back to New York," I said. "Drive me back to my car."

"It was just a joke," he repeated.

"Pretty lousy one."

"You feel that way, you drive back. I'll walk back along the flats."

"That's all right with me."

He got out. I moved over to the driver's seat. Turning the car around, I looked back and saw Viola and Martha standing in the doorway. Their broad grins were also fading into a look of perplexity.

* * *

It was not the kind of memory that I kept. It was painful to me personally and did not jibe with the normal character of Morgan. He wrote me a long letter of apology, using as excuses his morose mood and an excess of drinking. There was one aspect of the incident that had interested and amused me. He knew that I would go to the Cape on the slim basis of a postcard. He had made arrangements for an involved practical joke with the certainty that I would arrive to participate. Though he knew how to motivate me, he apparently misjudged my reactions.

I was astonished to note that it was well after one o'clock when I finished the first carton. I dreaded continuing.

Eight

I WASN'T SURPRISED WHEN I RECEIVED A MESSAGE THE next morning that I should call Operator 61 in New York City. Along with the telephone number of *View Magazine*, there was a name on the call-back slip. I should ask for Lester Price.

The first time I met Les was at lunch with Morgan. It was a Greek restaurant, off the beaten path for newspaper and magazine people. I liked it because it was quiet and gave me a chance to feel quietly important—one of the waiters had somehow discovered my name and remembered always to greet "Mr. Leeds." Morgan didn't like the food, but he sometimes met me there if I insisted.

Les came in that day, glanced around the main room, saw Morgan, and came at us with his right hand extended as if it were dragging him. "Morgan, Morgan, Morgan Stimmes! I'll be goddamned if it isn't Morgan Stimmes!"

I didn't like him. There was something of the bookkeeper about his face, gray white, rimless glasses glistening over dead gray eyes. His blackish brown hair was lacquered down in precise, oddly individual straight lines from a perfect part. The anxious glad-hand manner was totally out of keeping with his appearance.

We met on several other occasions—all without significance, just meetings and all in the company of Morgan. When I asked Morgan what Price did for a living, he would answer, "Some editorial job somewhere. I met him in Egypt. I think he was with UP or maybe it was AP. A year here, a year there, he's worked everywhere. I gave up asking him."

Now I knew. He was with *View*, or so the message indicated. However, my assumption was only partially right. We arranged to have dinner together in New York.

When I asked him what he was doing at *View*, he cackled and explained archly that he was providing a consulting service in sensitive matters.

"I'm a sensitive matter?" I asked.

"You might say that."

As there was no surprise that someone representing *View* called me, there was no surprise that Les opened our conversation that evening with a brusque "What the hell are you trying to do by sending tapes all over town?"

"You should have come to my apartment last night," I answered, feeling amused by his blunt accusation, "and you could have heard my answer to George Teagarten."

"George who?"

"Teagarten."

"Teagarten." He was momentarily speechless, his pale face crinkling slightly around his eyes; his eyes seemed to be gripping his glasses.

"I think I'd like a drink," I said, again guiltily remembering Touse's admonition about alcohol. I wondered if I should call Touse and tell him about these meetings. "Join me?"

"Sure," he said without enthusiasm.

We were at Kup's. The photographs of the uniformed men that plastered the walls when Morgan and I first drank there had been replaced by Broadway personalities. The grins were wide and toothy; success was wonderful. Nothing else had changed.

"Why did Teagarten go to see you? He wasn't supposed to."

"Who said he wasn't supposed to?"

"You're dead, Ken, if you sent those tapes."

"Why were you surprised by Teagarten?"

"I really didn't think that Teagarten would have gone to see you. He told me he wouldn't." His tight lips were pursed, as though sucking on sour frustration. His voice was more shrill; the petulant note of a child betrayed by a friend. "What did you tell Teagarten?"

"I told him the truth."

"On that evasion, we better have a drink."

I smiled. I didn't feel that I had any reason to take him seriously. Obviously, *View* and Brenther's had been approached by the same men. I felt sorry for him that his task in talking to me had already been accomplished. He would have a hard time in justifying his usefulness to his employers.

As I turned to catch the eye of a waiter, I looked into

the eyes of a thin-faced man sitting at the bar. The face holding the eyes turned abruptly toward the bartender. I didn't recognize the man.

As the evening progressed, ordering many rounds of drink—many more than I could remember—I knew that I had drunk too much. But Les had drunk more. He seemed greedy to obtain more glassware, more olives, more martinis. I'm sure we ate dinner.

Several times he repeated a statement that he had thrown in while first discussing Teagarten. Each time it was out of place. It was like a thought he had that he wanted on the record because he believed it was effective. It was like an echo. "You're dead, Ken, if you sent those tapes." He even said it after I explained that I hadn't sent the tapes. Perhaps he didn't believe me.

The evening ended when he leaned toward me, holding knuckle-white on the edge of the table as though he might slip off his seat if he didn't have a hard grip. "You know . . . I know . . . we . . . ought . . . I mean . . . we ought to t-t-team up and send tapes t-t-oooo the bastards . . . scare the bejesus out of them. Might, might pick up some dough . . . you got anything against dough?" He wiped his mouth quickly with the back of his hand and held onto the table again to keep himself from lurching. His grin of teeth disappeared behind pressed worried lips. "We'd be d-d-d-dead if they knew we sent those tapes." Everything was whispered.

I rose from the table unsteadily. His eyes were still fixed on the area where my face had been. He'll never miss me, I thought. I left, grateful to find the night air with a chill. Filling my lungs, I slowly regained an awareness of the difference between drunkenness and sobriety. I wanted sobriety and seemingly regained it mentally. My legs, however, were wobblingly beyond thought.

The following morning, awakened by the phone ringing, I suddenly realized that I had left my car in a parking lot in New York and had taken a taxi all the way to Connecticut. My God, I wondered what it cost me.

"Where in hell did you go last night?" said an irate Les.

"Did you miss me?"

"Tell you the truth, I didn't."

"Look," I said, "I didn't send the tapes. I don't know who did. As far as I'm concerned, the book will turn out to be a harmless revisit to another era. On that basis, will *View* pick up its contract with Stimmes?" I didn't know any quicker way of summing up and also giving Les some release from his own ineptitude at bargaining. I assumed this was what he wanted.

"I can't make bargains," he said. I must have made it too easy. He sounded as though I had exposed my neck to his razor and he was considering whether to cut.

"I think it might interest you to know that the gentlemen who received the tapes have an interest in seeing the story printed on the basis I just mentioned. Frankly, I don't have a hell of a lot to say to you unless you represent *View*. I'm only doing you a favor because you were Morgan's friend!"

Without toughness, he repeated, "I can't make bargains. I'm just not in a position to make them. You'll have to talk to someone else on the contract."

"Have that someone call me," I said, feeling more comfortable.

"I will," he said. There was no arrogance in him now.

"You can tell him that I'm looking for a writer to do the book. A writer from *View* might be just right."

He agreed again. Then he asked, "Have you ever met a skinny guy named Nick who was a friend of Stimmes?"

"No one comes to mind."

"Funny," he said, "I never had either until last night. He took me home and lifted my wallet. I don't think I'd ever recognize him again, except I know he was skinny. Goddamn embarrassing. Alcohol never hit me as it did last night. I still feel as if I'd been doped."

After I hung up I did remember the man at the bar staring at me. Was he skinny? I asked myself. It was a chilly feeling, remembering the strange eyes. Then I grinned. I was becoming suspicious of every event, of every person, even of a stranger at a bar. Even as I found amusement at this change in my character, I also began to wonder at my own deepening sense of being threatened. It was as though I were a child and were facing the unseen terrors of night on a gloomed country road. I was expecting every thicket to hold a nameless carnivorous monster.

After the class was over and I wandered out of the building, I was astonished to see Herman Touse sitting in a relaxed bulky sprawl on the top step.

"Waiting for me?"

He smiled and rose effortlessly to greet me. "I went to your office, but you never came. A secretary told me that

I could probably catch you after your class. And here you are."

"And here I am."

"Do you have a minute?" It was an unnecessary question, for he beckoned me to sit down on the steps at the same time. He didn't look at me. He stared out over the campus as he talked. "Your behavior concerns me," he said. "I caught an early morning flight when I heard about last night."

"What happened last night?"

"Your meeting with Lester Price. You drank too much."

"How the hell did you know?"

"At the moment the important question is not how I knew. What was discussed? What was said?"

At first I was angry. I didn't answer.

"Please," he said, "don't feel that I'm tampering. I think you are in a web, you know. I don't know whether it's a dangerous one or not. I suspect it isn't but I don't want to take chances. I don't want you to take chances."

I considered his words, wondering how I should take them. Was he serious? Then I recalled how Stimmes had trapped me originally into agreeing to the chore of having the book published after he died. Was that the web he was referring to?

I told him about the evening before and the call from Price in the morning.

He nodded wisely. "Do you consider yourself naïve?" he asked. He was now looking at me.

"I don't think anyone would admit to believing himself naïve." I laughed.

"I think you are in some respects."

"In what respects?"

"Last night's performance was certainly naïve. Fortunately, Mr. Price is incompetent. You certainly are when it comes to Mrs. Stimmes. I think she is something evil." He noted my reaction to the strong words. "Evil is a rather strong way to describe her, but Morgan Stimmes certainly conveyed to me the idea of evil. I have yet to measure this against experience."

"Confusion?"

"Some about her. Stimmes suggested in a letter to me that I should accept the letter E as short for evil. Then he alway referred to his wife as E. Stimmes. My impression was that Elizabeth Stimmes was evil. I think he was too good a writer not to want us to have this particular kind of impression."

"If you got an impression of evil, he was trying to give it to you. I agree."

"Good. Incidentally, I lost his ashes. They've disappeared."

"I'd think his wife would have them." I smiled. I couldn't understand why the ashes had importance.

"That's possible, but I wasn't able to trace them to her. I had assumed that I would be able to follow their progress. There's no pleasure for a lawyer to lose the slightest control of a situation."

"It doesn't sound too serious unless you suspected he was still alive."

"I am almost completely certain that he is dead. That's not the problem. I just keep wondering why the link should break. It makes me think that there is a reason I should know. There's one other thing that worries me."

"Just one?"

He chortled. "My concern will also answer your first question about how I knew about last night. Interested?"

"Interested."

"I've had you followed. It's quite a standard procedure with me. I always hire a private detective. He called me in the early morning to tell me about last night." His eyes studied me for a reaction. "My detective also told me something that disturbed me. Someone else is also following you." His eyes never left me.

I wasn't sure that I owed him a reaction. I didn't like the idea of being followed by his detective or by any other detective. There was something ridiculous about learning that there was a parade of people following you. But I wasn't amused.

"At first," he continued, "I was inclined to think that my man was building up the story, trying to give me my money's worth. Last night, apparently, the other man drove you home in a stolen taxi. He abandoned it in Rye."

"Good God!" I let escape. "I don't even know what the driver looks like."

"Charitable soul, I would gather," he said. "You were in pretty sad condition."

"Pretty sad."

"You don't remember anything about him?"

"I remember vaguely the identification picture, but you say the man driving wasn't the one on the picture."

"Not the same."

"How does your man describe him?"

"Not very articulate, I'm afraid. Chunky, short. I wonder why anyone else is following you."

"Why the hell were you having me followed?"

"I wanted to make sure you were the type to stay out of trouble. Also, I was curious about some of the curiosities of Stimmes' rules."

"Like what?"

"An example? I am to send you a bottle of wine after arrangements for his book are completed, with a note reading, 'There is always another bottle.' Meaningful?"

I laughed. "Really not very curious. It dates back to the very first conversation I had with Morgan."

"I was also never to admit sending it to you."

"You shouldn't be telling me now."

He winked. "Unless I found it necessary to tell you in order to explain my odd arrangements with him."

"You're kidding?" Morgan's weird sense of humor had stunned me. I found it almost unbelievable that anyone could have conceived of such an intricate joke.

"I told you that I have very curious rules. Do you want my opinion?"

I nodded.

"Mr. Stimmes had something quite different in mind and found in your readiness to perform some acts one means of accomplishing it. I think you have a role to perform. It was a lark at first. I sensed that Mr. Stimmes had incorporated you into an elaborate plot. It was like seeing a play, watching each act unfold. It was quite fascinating. First I watched the body and saw it disappear. It was a magic act."

"This is the truth, isn't it?"

"Every word."

"I think it's weird, the whole business." I said, "It must be some kind of joke, and I don't understand the punch line. All I know is that there are two guys out there, each probably reporting on the other. Morgan must have thought that was funny in itself. Let's forget about the one you hired. Remove yours. There's no point in paying for a joke no one will laugh at. Anyway, I find it damn embarrassing having you know everything about me."

He didn't look pleased. He finally shrugged his shoulders. "Perhaps you're right," he said.

Nine

ON THURSDAY MORNING I RECEIVED A LETTER FROM Elizabeth. In a childish scrawl, obviously written hastily, it said: "Don't forget Friday. I need you whether you're any good or not." Her signature was interesting. It was as simple as her note—just E.

By evening I had put Elizabeth in a corner of my mind, not to be considered until the next day. Interestingly, another anxiety had receded. At first, after talking to Touse, I spent a considerable amount of time glancing over my shoulder or spinning around quickly to see if I could see my follower. My lack of success in finding anyone who seemed to be interested in my movements finally eroded my interest. I decided that Touse's detective was gone and with him had disappeared the other one, apparently belonging to no one in particular.

There was no word from Les Price or from anyone from *View*. I decided I'd call Touse Monday and let him set up any negotiations that were necessary. And so I removed that, too, from my mind.

Thursday night I tackled Stimmes' cartons again. With some apprehension that I would suffer from boredom, I ensconced myself in a collection of pillows on the bed, with a cup of hot coffee on a side table, the contents of one box next to me. In truth, I expected sleep to overcome me before I had made much progress. But Morgan had a surprise for me.

After I removed the files I noticed that the bottom of the carton had no seams. As I began to leaf through the papers and files looking for something that would hold my interest, I wondered why a simple cardboard carton didn't show separations where the four edges folded together. I picked the box off the floor. Upside down the divisions of the folds were there.

Tricky bastard, I said to myself. He has pasted a sheet of brown paper very neatly inside. Without ceremony I ripped the paper off. Underneath I found several sheets of typescript. I had a sense of excitement and a glowing knowledge of my own brilliance. I also had admiration for Morgan's uses of subterfuge. There was something eerie about knowing that Morgan had devised means of communicating after death. Somewhere in that strange marriage of his to Elizabeth there was a corner of accumulated hatreds and suspicions that made all of this necessary. I marveled at the force of the venom that had a man like him spend an evening carefully cutting brown paper and pasting it in the bottom of a box.

"Leeds," the note began.

Fantastic, I thought. Morgan knew that I would find the notes. What monumental certainty!

> It is often difficult to determine how successful an undertaking is going to be, no matter how much time and effort is put in planning. This note will deal with your present involvement. (I apologize for not being frank with you in the beginning. I'm sure you suspected I was planning something, but being a good sort you nodded and blundered on. Please continue blundering. There are rewards, Leeds, even if they only seem to be internal ones of doing favors for the dead.)
>
> By this time you will have made contact with *View* and Brenther's. Correct?

Correct, I mumbled. "Blundering" offended me. I wondered why he used a word that gave me the feeling that he was being contemptuous. I continued reading.

> And unless I'm gravely (no pun intended) wrong, you have slept with my wife. Being dead when you read this, I think there is nothing morally wrong with your behavior. It is quite natural for both of you. (Being alive when I write this, I'm livid with rage at the thought. What a terrible confusion to attempt to be both dead and alive simultaneously!) If anything has prevented this natural consummation of passion—knowing you, I know there are threads in your life having to do with virtue and moral dilly-dally balled around a spindle of do and don't that will torture you to an early grave—put it aside and consummate. Your dealings with Elizabeth will be easier if you spend a few evenings in her bed. She is less complicated in bed and

tends to take this simpler form of life into her out-of-bed world for a short time.

Dealings with Elizabeth? As you will have already discovered, Elizabeth is far more intricate than she seems. No matter how careful I will be that these cartons do not fall into her hands, she will have them. I know this. I assume she will trade her body for them. It won't be comfortable knowledge for you when you share her bed, but she will have paid an extremely demeaning price. Only of that I can be certain. I can't guess at the price she will ask you to pay. You may not pay it immediately, but she will make you pay. All I can say on this score, friend, is Good Luck.

I presume you have now met Touse. This complicated world of yours was created by overpopulation and lawyers. Large masses of people naturally found individuals to make road signs. Lawyers made these signs so complicated it took other lawyers to explain them to the masses, and so it goes. Touse knows the way better than any lawyer I have ever met. However, his talent for simplification is dangerous. I want you to use his advice, but I caution you to use it wisely. Weigh it carefully. He will lie on occasion to motivate you. This in itself is harmless as long as you remain wary and behave as you deem best and natural. You'll like Touse until he makes you feel you're involved in some complicated plot. Touse sees plots and schemes in the simplest of transactions at the greengrocer. I will guess that my desire to provide for my son and eliminate Elizabeth from the book profits has set Touse spinning webs. There are no webs other than those he spins.

Since I first spoke to you about the Wester book, I have found a writer who would be ideal to do the writing. I barely know him, I have read little of what he has written. But he's a gem in that he knows the era. I think he'll be willing to take on the project.

Because Touse spins, here's flax for him. I have given him the writer's name and address. Wrote him that he is not to tell you the name unless you ask. I wonder what he'll make of this. (This wonderment I leave behind me. If I'm not careful, I find that I can sit for hours wondering what will happen to every person, wondering how this or that situation will unravel. It's a morbid game leading to only one human conclusion: tears and fruitless prayers.)

Forgive me for being discursive for a sentence or two. I have found that I enjoy writing for the first time in my life. Why did I ever begin to write? I presume I was interested in attracting young women who thought writers were sensitive beings with something special to offer in the sack. A prestigious line of work! I suppose the reasons were wrong, for I have bled over every word I have placed on paper. Each has scissored at my entrails. Now! When all hope is gone, words pour from me in gushing lovely spatters of gaudy-colored unthinking lurid watery ease. The scissor slits are healed, and I bleed no more. Perhaps the blood is gone because there is no more hope.

It would be a fine gesture for you to see my son. It might be a protective device if his mother were to know that someone was still interested in his future. There is a loneliness, I think, in being adrift in a family, especially in a family that views you as a foreign body. Poor lad! He might turn out as an interesting person, having a fascinating background. Or, more likely, he will become a craven adult, cowering from his future. Ask Touse for his address and mother's name. He has instructions to give this information to you when you request it. (More flax for Touse, who spins.)

I realized that Morgan had created a rationale to allay my suspicions if I had suspicions. He was being very logical; in his apparent candidness, he was telling me that he was catering to Touse's desire to see plots. Was he really perpetrating an elaborate joke on a lawyer? Or was I the victim? In any case, he had made me a victim of my own uncertainty.

Do you remember visiting me on the Cape? I've never really apologized enough to your satisfaction for my behavior on that occasion. I still can't honestly, because I still think it was funny. You acted very badly. I've never understood why you became so upset. At this moment I find I'm beginning to giggle when I think of that day. Damn it, Leeds, it was funny!

The arrangements made for the few kind words—I have odd notions about kindness—made over my urn have not included invitations to the two women you met on the Cape. Names: Viola Grafton and Martha Kempton. I'm writing Touse to find their addresses. No instructions other than he should have a means of finding them because you might want to write or telephone them. I was forgetful when I compiled the list of those I want to attend my urn-ash-word ritual. (It's not *my* ritual, is it? It was never done over my ashes before.)

I'm probably wrong in my estimate of when you will find these sheets of paper. But I'm counting on your perceptive intelligence. If I'm right, you'll get an invitation within the next few days. I know you, Leeds. I think I do. This is one of the great satisfactions of death. As I wait for my escort to lead me from here, I've made the very pleasant discovery that I can make judgments that are unmuddled by personal considerations. How often emotion-ego has forced me to posture stupidly and behave inanely! I see you and Touse and Elizabeth with vivid clarity. Oh, God, how funny! How funny it is to know for the first time. I want to finish this section of the notes, but I'm broken with laughter. I'm saying things outside of the typewriter that I can't put down. You wouldn't understand. There is madness in all of us. I sometimes think you knew about the child. I hope that's obscure. I don't want to type this over.

And the note ended abruptly. Coherence was apparently leaving Morgan as he wrote. I rose from the bed and stretched. I knew that each of the cartons contained notes to me. Morgan didn't have to footnote that information. He knew me, all right. I was now worried. And as I worried I wondered if Morgan had not known that I would be worried. I was a Yo-Yo at a point in space trying to determine whether I was spinning up or down. What would happen if I called Touse and read him the letter? If I were Touse, I would feel offended at being toyed with. I would know, after hearing these words, that Morgan was playing games. I'd refuse to play the game.

Where would that leave me? Touse's interest would disappear. He would kick himself for wasting money. I'd be alone. If there were a plot, I would be caught in it in lonely splendor. In my smallest voice I said, "Help."

I hated Morgan Harper Stimmes. I wished him alive so that I could wish him dead.

Frenzied by frustration, I dumped each of the cartons and ripped off the brown paper. I wasn't wrong. There was a letter waiting for me in each. "Help," I said again aloud in a small voice. And the sound was funny. I felt absurd. But I also felt afraid. Even the room seemed threatening. But it was funny that I felt afraid.

"I can't call Touse," I said to myself. As I made that decision I knew that Morgan had really made it for me.

The notes from the cartons spread before me, my face burning hot with the frustrations of anger, I lowered myself to the edge of the bed. My back ached, and I told myself that I had sat too long already.

What the hell, Leeds! It's a short trip and it's not so damn merry, but it is a trip. I have a confession. You have disturbed me ever since we first met. As with most people, I have the little man inside of me who keeps saying that I'm a great man. As with most people, I shout back in the middle of the night, "Prove it, you little bastard! I want to believe it!" But he's quiet. You, Leeds, are my outside little bastard. Somehow you convinced me that you think that I am a great man. But then you'd carve into my character in some way as though molding me into what you wanted to believe I am. It would hurt like hell. It bewildered me to see that you didn't totally accept my perfection. And then I'd ask my inside little bastard to prove that I was the embodiment of perfection. The little bastard wouldn't say a word. He was on your side. His silence was eloquent. The silence usually lasted a number of days, only ending after I gave up asking the question.

Now, sitting here, plopping down on handfuls of typewriter keys, slugging down a quart of my best, knowing that Elizabeth is awake in the bedroom listening to my hammering keys, I've decided to lay away both little bastards.

I don't give a damn about perfection any longer. I know I'm not a great man and know that I will never be. When you read this I'm a dead man. At this moment you don't know how happy this makes me feel. Never again will I worry about your scalpel making thin slices, or your sewing needle. I'm free of you, Leeds. I will never again look into your shining bright admiring eyes and see disappointment. I will never again be a tarnished hero. Never, never, never, never, never, never again!

I have a mad thought that would make existence a complete pleasure. If we could only reverse everything in time. We would then be plucked from the grave—the mortician becomes a heroic body finder and the giver of life—and we would grow younger and stronger rather than enfeebled and senile. Think on how wonderful wars would be when soldiers march out to use weapons that draw bullets from the dead so that the dead might live. Each war would end with more alive. Limbs would be sewed on rather than removed. Think of the gaiety. Think of the mysteries that this would inspire. Indeed, one could believe in a God or in an Olympus full of them.

The only thing wrong would be the inevitable ways of humans. Because the finding of bodies would be so important, people would dig the world into a large pit, mining corpses.

Enough of this. Every pleasant thought ends in misery.

I hear Elizabeth stirring. Trot, trot she goes, down the hall to the kitchen. She paused a moment by my door as if she were about to interrupt, but I fooled her by continuing to type. Aha, she says to herself, he is still working. I hear her still moving about. Like a child, she is creating noise enough to pique the curiosity of her elders. Christ! What is she doing?

Did you know that young women who marry older men tend to begin aging themselves by wearing their hair in buns, using less make-up, walking with less grace, buying tweeds. All their husbands wanted were vivacious, sexy creatures; all they finally had were women who appeared in all ways as old as themselves. I would like to see Elizabeth with a young man, for I've seen her age faster than a warm grape.

Perhaps women are naturally old. I hear her again. Softly

she comes. She hesitates by my door. Will she enter, even though she hears the typewriter? I doubt it. She has some strange respect for the sound of click clack, and I now click clack as rapidly as this ancient machinery will allow. The sound frightens her because it means that a human being is trying to be productive. Productivity scares her. I think she equates it with some God impulse. I recognized this in her long ago and have used it to advantage in creating moments of peace for myself. She will never know as you have always suspected that productivity is foreign to me. I have always faked it, knowing that it's socially useful to be known as a productive person. Do you remember when we first met? Burning from your eyes was the immediate knowledge that I was a fraud. I had a choice. I could have walked from your closet of a room and forgotten you and the stinking job I never got. We probably would never have seen one another again. Instead, I was challenged by your stare and proceeded to create the great man. To my horror, I charmed you into an illusion of my productivity, and we became friends.

She's gone. Much more quiet in the going than the coming! When she wants to make noise, she scrapes her feet. When retreating and quiet, she lifts them, and all I hear are the gentle sounds of her body whispering through space. Oh, my God! I paused for a moment to listen and can hear her breathing. She is still there, listening. All of my imagined whispering is wrong. My mind is suddenly blank. I don't know what to type. Because she is there and is still listening. The moment I stop she will be inside with me. I feel panic. There is nothing more to write now.

Morgan had gone mad, I decided. Again he had shaken me up with a letter. My skin was pouted with goose bumps, and my eyes hurt from staring pointlessly into the space of the room. I had suddenly become a villain. Now I could review every moment with Morgan and see my villainy. I was appalled by this twist. It could have been amusing had I not once admired Morgan. With that very admiration as his weapon, he had impaled me. Did he really believe what he had written? Or had he woven me deeper into his dark fabric?

Remembering the first time I had met Elizabeth, her strange unacceptance of his impending death, I wondered now if she had not been his first victim. I felt sympathy for her behavior now. Though not knowing precisely how he set up her behavior on that ghastly occasion, I firmly believed that he had manipulated her.

Perhaps he was even describing the method in this last letter by closing himself from her, keeping the typewriter rattling away until the early morning. I remembered his voice, its rasping quality, and her words that she preferred it with a normal quality. Perhaps it wasn't a callous comment. He might have been faking, and she was simply making an observation. I must ask her, I decided.

There is a sweetness in the night air, Leeds. It is four o'clock in the morning, and I've opened the window. Even here in the Village at this hour, there is a notable silence. I admit I can hear a man sobbing somewhere in the darkness, a woman shrilling to a companion while she pounds her high steels into the concrete. There is a horn. Oddly, these sounds are part of the quiet, as if without them there would be no quiet.

What is there about the early morning that makes a man reflective? I suppose the urgencies of the day no longer press. It's gliding time.

How about a game played while you live and after I die? It will give me a few weeks of immortality, a time when I have a place on this Earth, even though my body will have no active role and take no space. Ghoulish?

A Roman horse goes trot and then trot again. You're off and running. The game is on.

Ten

I LAY AWAKE FOR SEVERAL HOURS, FORGETTING FOR A time those of Morgan's letters that made sense in that they contained words and sentences and thoughts. I was bewildered by the rest of them that had only random letters, unspaced, incomprehensible. They were total nonsense. Morgan's mind was not apparently functioning as a leader to his fingers.

What else but pure nonsense could a line reading *infomtomethelybddlllerrilnberc y smamqummbnercdingemedndergci* be? It occurred to me that he had begun his game by coding the rules. I struggled for an hour before sleep, trying to puzzle the code, scribbling out the sensible inside words like "in" "to" "me" "the" and gave up because I came out with meaningless phrases without nouns or verbs. The only interesting thing I could note, assuming it was pure accidental falling of fingers on typewriter keys, was the large number of "me's" that were on the pages. It was probably Morgan keeping Elizabeth at bay by keeping his typewriter clattering.

None of the stereotype phrases was apt. I felt no prickling on the back of my neck. Nothing compelled me to turn. I glanced into a window display of shoes, thinking that it was time to buy another pair because I had already had the pair I was wearing reheeled, resoled, reheeled, and resoled too many times. As my eyes moved toward a rear pair, I was aware of the reflection in the glass of the street behind me.

And there he was, standing nonchalantly across the street by a disposal wire basket. I suppose Touse's telling me that I had been followed gave me the instant knowledge that I was seeing my follower. He was by reflection a chubby man, quite short. I judged that he had on an overcoat rather than the more seasonal topcoat, for he had a hand stuffed in a straight-across bulky pocket.

I was more amused than angry or disturbed by his presence. It was as though I had been expecting to see him, so that when I did, I wasn't surprised. I wondered how I might turn and see him so that I could recognize him in the future. I didn't want to frighten him away. And most of all I didn't want him to realize that I knew he was there.

I reached into my pocket and took out my cigarettes. As I turned toward the street I began to light up, briefly looking up. He was not a terribly good detective. As casual as he seemingly was in the reflection, he was intently staring at me. His eyes—like the coal eyes of a snowman—were unblinkingly directed at me.

As brief as the description provided by Touse was, it was accurate. My follower was chunky and short. He was the mystery one, not Touse's. Obviously, detectives played roles; this man wanted people to know he worked as a detective. There was an air about him that exuded his odd part: the winter coat, drawn up to his chin, a hat with the brim drawn down. There was a sort of unkempt devil-may-care toughness about him. A lumpy face, deeply creased, wallowed with a ruddy exuberance around prominent unblinking eyes.

I began walking, pleased with myself that I now could identify him wherever I saw him. At this moment I felt no intrusion into my personal life. I wasn't, after all, doing anything clandestine; I had no reason to attempt to seek seclusion. I felt almost flattered that anyone would find my actions of interest. In fact, I was almost pleased to have a companion.

However, I thought it was time to find out who he was and why he was following me. I had almost an hour before the next and last class of the day. After it was over I intended to head for New York to see Elizabeth.

Entering a drugstore at the corner, I bought a pack of cigarettes and then tucked myself into the phone booth. I called Touse's office in Washington. I called collect, and it was accepted.

"I'm sorry but Mr. Touse is not in at the moment. I expect him in about a half-hour," said a sweet secretarial voice. "Is something urgent?" she asked.

I told her, "Yes."

She took the number of the phone in the drugstore and told me that I would hear from Touse within five minutes.

I made another trip to the counter and bought a package of razor blades. Glancing through the front door, I noted that my man was standing just to the side of the entrance, looking at a display. While my change was being made, the phone rang.

Touse apologized for not being in his office when I called, and I broke in: "The man shadowing me is outside the drugstore. I thought this would be a good time to find out who he is. Do you still have your detective?"

"I canceled him as I said I would."

"I guess I shouldn't have been so quick to ask you to get rid of him. I suppose I can walk up to this guy and ask him point-blank why he's following me."

Touse laughed. "I think there's a better way of finding out about him."

"I'm open to suggestions."

"I'll have the police pick him up for stealing a cab. This way you won't be involved."

I gave him a complete description of the man and the location of the drugstore.

"It won't take very long," he promised me.

Fortunately, drugstores have grown into broad diversionary areas. Buying a magazine, I then went to the fountain and ordered a cup of coffee. I hoped it wouldn't take long; my class met in thirty minutes. It would take me five minutes to get there. I didn't dare to look outside, so I buried myself in the magazine.

"Sir."

I looked up to see the man from behind the drug counter. "Yes?" I said.

"You forgot your change when you answered the telephone."

I looked at him sheepishly as I collected my change.

"And your blades."

"Thanks," and I also took a small paper bag.

The commotion outside was loud enough to hear inside. Everyone turned to look.

The man was complaining, "What the hell have I done?" He was leaning forward off balance with his two hands against the glass window. "You got no right!" One policeman was running his hands down his body while the other stood back holding a service revolver. "I tell you that you got no right!"

The policeman frisking him pulled an automatic from inside the man's jacket. "I got a license. I got a right to carry that!" As far as I could hear, the policemen weren't speaking.

"Looks like a tough bird," said the druggist at my elbow. "Wonder what he's done?"

"Watch the coat! You're gonna get in a jam over this. I swear!" And it was swiftly over. The closest policeman had the man's coat balled up between the shoulder blades and was shoving him toward the street.

"That was quick," said the druggist.

I agreed, tossed a dime on the counter to pay for my coffee, and left.

At a quarter of five I pulled into a gas station en route to New York. I called Touse. He was back in the office.

"You know who the guy is?" I asked.

"John Sayles. He seems to be the man who stole the taxi. He works for a small detective agency that does some industrial spying and some New York divorce work. I think it might be of some interest to you that his one phone call was used to call his office in New York to say that he couldn't finish up by being in the Village this evening."

"Is that supposed to mean something to me?"

"I guessed that you were probably going to see Mrs. Stimmes this evening."

"That's right."

"I think that you've been set up for something this evening. Since this obviously is not a divorce action, Stimmes being dead, I think it might be dangerous for you."

"What kind of danger would there be?"

"I don't know. I can't even guess. It just looks peculiar—peculiar enough to be somewhat frightening."

"Did you find out anything else about Sayles?"

"I wasn't exactly in the position of having the police make a specific inquiry. They were nice enough to give me this much information. I have, however, rehired my detective to look into the matter."

I didn't speak, thinking rapidly about Stimmes' notes that I had read.

"Ken?" Touse asked anxiously in the silence. "You still there?"

"Still here. I was on my way into the city to have dinner with Elizabeth."

"Do you think that's wise?"

"How do I know if it's wise," I snapped.

"Has anything else happened?"

"I found some messages from Stimmes in the cartons."

"I see."

"You see what?"

He laughed. "I think something is going to happen tonight. Perhaps not. I'm fascinated in following Stimmes' twists and turns. In any case, I'm flying into New York and will be at my office there. I would like to see the messages. Do you think I can see them this evening? Can you bring them to my office?"

"Do you think they're important?"

"They might have a different importance to me than they have for you."

"I'll have to go back home to get them." I glanced at my watch. "Sure. I don't know what time I'll get to your office. It might be late. Remember. Elizabeth."

"Don't worry about the time. I'll be waiting for you."

Elizabeth had grown more beautiful. I wondered—remembering Morgan's written comment about women aging themselves for older men—if she had not begun to demonstrate her youth. She looked very virginal, if it's possible to describe a woman in that state in more than yes or no terms. My belief that this was to be an ominous evening wisped away as if it were morning fog and she was the sun. I was delighted.

She stood in the open door without speaking. Studying me for a brief moment, she looked approving. Then she spun around to show me how she looked. "Do you like?" she asked as she turned.

I grinned. I searched for words to express my liking but she didn't require any. She leaped forward, putting her arms around my neck, and kissed me. "See what I've done!" Taking my hands, she tugged me into her apartment.

She had been busy. Stimmes' furniture, the hall mirror, the carpets were gone. The walls were now cocoa-colored, filled with glowing creamy paintings. A new telephone table. A new chair. Gleaming with polish. She pulled me through the rooms; small sentences of joy burst from her. She had removed everything that had belonged to Stimmes and had replaced it. The new pieces were light, seemingly balanced delicately on narrow tapered rods. The entire apartment was flaming with new additional paintings. I even touched one—it was so shining. I was surprised it was dry. The apartment no longer belonged to Morgan. The earlier changes had been just the beginning.

"Now you must take me somewhere so we can drink wine."

"How on earth could you afford to do all this?" I blurted.

"To be alive is to be rich," she answered and pranced to the closet near the door and plucked a light blue coat from inside.

Even in my enchantment with her, I remained troubled. As we sat in a small restaurant nearby that she had suggested, she noticed that I was not totally responsive to her gaiety. "Are you tired?" she asked.

"A little," I answered truthfully.

"There's something bothering you."

"The kind of wine I should order."

She brightened. "A champagne." She watched my face. "I'll pay," she said. "I know you can't afford it."

"That bothers me."

"Then you pay."

"How on earth can you possibly afford to pay for anything?" I finally allowed the question to escape.

Fortunately, the waiter came at this moment. Her face was clouded. The brightness of her eyes dulled. She seemed to show no interest in the menu, so I ordered for the two of us. She did not object. The waiter flinched when I asked him about champagne. He said he'd check on the supply and thought that he could find some Piper-Heidseick.

When he had gone, Elizabeth reached across the table and took my hands in hers. "I am rich, you know. I am not proud of my father, but he did accumulate much money. He was an immoral man. Morgan was too, you know. He and I often fought about his admiration for my father. I received a letter from Morgan after he died; it must have been posted by a nurse at the hospital. All it said—and I'm certain Morgan wanted me to feel guilt—was that Claude Wester, my father, was a great man and that I should love my father.

"Morgan thought I didn't want him to write a book about my father. I really didn't care, but he raged at me and kept saying that I was a disloyal daughter. I think sometimes that Morgan thought he was my father. They were so much alike I sometimes thought of them as being one." She pressed my hands tightly. "Are you still troubled?"

"One question! Do you feel detached from the events of Morgan's death? Do you feel anything about him?"

"I felt lost for a time," she replied. "But I don't feel anything now. I've become so annoyed with the little games he arranged after his death that I have almost hated him."

"Games?"

"I'm certain he wanted to punish me. I found funny little notes all around the apartment telling me to do this or that. Those boxes you have were part of the game. I followed them as if they were important. I had a small package in the apartment that I had to deliver to a minister. Oh, darling, I'm so tired of his games."

"After dinner I'd like you to go with me to see Touse in his office. You see, I've been playing games too. So has Morgan's lawyer. Tonight would be a good time for all of us to find out what each of us is doing." And so I made the decision. As long as I believed that Elizabeth was the evil force Morgan described, I would be powerless.

Looking across the table, feeling the pressure of her small tense hands, I felt guilty that I had ever considered her with Morgan's eyes. I wondered if the change of my emotions had been wrought by Elizabeth. Then instantly I knew that Morgan had made the change. Had I not read the messages the night before, I would have plodded forward with my suspicions.

I explained to Elizabeth that I had begun to feel that everything I felt and did now I could trace to Morgan. Even when I acted negatively to his stimulus, I had begun to believe that he had intended me to behave negatively.

"Even now, as we sit here? Do you think he expected you to invite me to that meeting tonight?" Her wan smile had a motherliness, a There-There look.

"At this moment? I guess I've learned to ask the question: Is Morgan driving me to this? I ask it when I do anything."

She laughed. "Poor darling."

I said it. "The hell with Morgan Harper Stimmes!"

She laughed louder.

It was pleasant to have a confederate. It felt a little strange to have my confederate be Morgan's widow, for I still had a notion that widows were almost more tied to their former husbands in death than in life.

Elizabeth was still laughing. The color of her cheeks was high, such as you might find on a schoolgirl running on a winter's day. Her eyes glittered gaily behind narrowed squeezed laughing openings.

"It's good to have you on my side," she finally said.

Touse—looking very much as a man named Herman should—rolled his head toward us as if it were on a runner. His sleepy eyes widened as he studied Elizabeth.

"Ah, Elizabeth! Elizabeth Stimmes! I'm delighted that Ken was thoughtful enough to bring you here. We now can be candid and see if we can understand what game your late husband has been playing with us."

"Perhaps I shouldn't be here," said Elizabeth, "but I think it's a good idea for all of us to speak to one another. I've lived with Morgan and know how involved people become with his life. And now apparently he has done the same with his death."

Touse was evidently unable to remove his eyes from her. His study of her showed no admiration. At the same time it could not be described as academic. She was being viewed by Touse much as I would view a new threatening food on my plate, wondering if it would taste good, wondering if it would be harmful. She was clearly an unordered chocolate-covered grasshopper.

"I have the feeling," answered Touse, "that he was a simple form of life. He has on occasion referred to himself as a dinosaur. I think he should have been congratulated for self-knowledge. As a dinosaur he was accustomed to casting a large shadow."

"It looks like more than a shadow right now," I added. "This business with detectives is real enough."

Elizabeth was shocked. "Detectives? I don't understand!"

"Mrs. Stimmes," declared Touse, "there is nothing to understand. Your late husband had you and Ken followed. The reason he had this done is not clear. Perhaps after this evening we might have a suggestion of an idea. I doubt if we will know why with any exactitude."

I was curious as to why Elizabeth seemed so upset. Touse's words didn't calm her.

Touse plunged on. At no time during the evening did he remove his eyes from Elizabeth for very long. Feeling uneasy, I accepted his invitation to have a drink.

"I think we might spend some time reading some of the

notes we have all received from the late Mr. Stimmes. I understand you have found some fresh notes, Ken."

I removed the folded papers from my inside pocket and handed the packet to him. "You can read them in almost any order," I commented.

"What are these?" Touse asked, holding up the papers with the random typing.

"Part of the notes." I glanced at Elizabeth, who had drawn up a chair near him. "Judging by some comments he made elsewhere, he was trying to convince Elizabeth he was hard at work. I could be wrong. For all I know, those pages are all in code."

Touse was looking at Elizabeth too; she smiled wanly at him.

As Elizabeth leaned over the papers, taking one sheet in hand, I said, "You'll find some of Morgan's comments tough to take."

"I expected that they would be," she replied, her lips tight and bloodless.

I watched their faces. I probably shouldn't have let Elizabeth see the pages. As Touse read, he handed the sheets of paper to Elizabeth.

I knew the reference instantly when I saw Touse's face color. He glanced at me a second and then at Elizabeth. This reaction could not have been stimulated by any other page than the one on which Morgan referred to Elizabeth and me sleeping together. I sipped at the whiskey, studying Touse. What would he do?

He handed the page to her as though it contained nothing that would concern her. As he read on, I noticed that his eyes flickered over at her. He was waiting for her reaction. It might have been funny if I, too, weren't worried about her reaction. I felt cruel, almost sadistic, in allowing it to be read by the two of them.

Elizabeth began to read. She smiled, looked up and caught Touse's eyes, then swung her head to see me. "He really was a louse, wasn't he?" she said without emotion.

"Could he have been insane?" I asked.

Touse answered, "There is no easy answer. I find it hard to believe that a man who planned so expertly could be insane. These are not random sentences. They are careful lies. You see, Mr. Stimmes never believed that you would allow us to read them. Certain things were placed so that they would militate against showing them to anyone. The comments about Mrs. Stimmes of a sexual nature. Would anyone but an uncouth lout allow them to be read by her or me? So you can be flattered. He did not think you would show them. He thought you would cooperate with him in his childish game involving you and me. Probably he thought you wouldn't dare tell me that it was only a game. It really is quite insulting to have a client such as Morgan Stimmes consider you an idiot."

"Have you read everything?" I asked.

"Not yet. However, you're very wise to let us read these pages. I wish I had brought the letters he wrote me," Touse said. "He makes it emotionally impossible to show letters to anyone else. He thoroughly insults Elizabeth, as he does here. He calls you a fag with intellectual qualities."

Elizabeth suddenly burst into laughter. She pointed a finger at me. "Do you remember," she asked, "that I asked you if you were a homosexual? My wonderful lying husband had me almost convinced that you were. I've wondered what you thought of me for asking such a terrible question. I didn't know how to explain that Morgan always referred to you as a gimpy fairy."

I think that now we were all amused by Morgan. The odd exotic air he had pumped up around our movements was gone. We had caught him at his game, and he looked ridiculous. He was a gray naked corpse dancing among the nettles. The tragedy had suddenly disappeared. It was a comedy, after all. It was a pleasant discovery for me, for I no longer felt the need to hate Morgan and suffer the subsequent guilt. Elizabeth seemed to sense the same thing.

But Touse wasn't smiling. He looked at each of our faces. He laid the papers down and stood up. We waited from him to speak. He sauntered across the room. He was an unlikely figure of a man delicately poling along on dainty feet. He finally ended up at his desk, opening the bottom left drawer where the liquor was kept. "A warm drink?" he asked.

I held out my paper cup. He looked disapprovingly as he poured an inch of bourbon. Then he did the same in another cup. "I agree with you all," he said. "It does seem comic all of a sudden. But I wonder." He let us both wonder, because he began to drink instead of talk. When he had finished the contents of his cup, he poured another for himself. "Morgan Harper Stimmes was never a comic," he continued. "He was, as he himself describes himself, a dinosaur. He was no vegetable-eating large lizard. He was a flesh eater. A flesh eater is never comic. I'm concerned that you are beginning to think of all this as a mere joke.

Perhaps I should tell you something about Morgan Harper Stimmes that you never knew. I took the trouble to find out that he was a notorious practical joker. I used the word 'notorious' advisedly. When he was a young man in Paris, he had made an odd practice of sending cablegrams to parents of friends announcing the death of those friends. Even after one of the parents who received the cable died of a heart attack, he continued. The newspapers took note when one of his friends tried to kill him."

"You have more examples?" I asked.

"Nothing quite as bizarre or as deadly, but more, yes."

"I'm beginning to wonder how I could have ever admired him," I said.

"Although I didn't bring any of Mr. Stimmes' notes with me, I did bring the material—addresses and such—that you are supposed to ask me for."

Touse handed me a crumpled paper. Everything was on it that Morgan had written to ask for. Viola Grafton and Martha Kempton now had an address and a telephone number. I was surprised. They lived together still and in the Village.

I could also get in touch with Morgan's illegitimate son. Next to the noun WRITER, Touse had scrawled *John Lupin.*

"I wonder why Mr. Stimmes went to all this trouble. I assumed that he had written you the questions, and me, the answers," Touse said and shook his head in puzzlement.

"He probably didn't want us to pay too much attention to either question or answer. I'd say he was flagging us with the game, hoping we wouldn't think too much about the pieces we were playing with," I guessed.

"I'm impressed," said Touse. "I think you are right."

It was after eleven when the phone rang. "Nick will be here in fifteen minutes," Touse announced on hanging up. "He's my detective. He says that there's a man covering Mrs. Stimmes' apartment." Touse grinned broadly. "They've lost contact. When Sayles was picked up in Connecticut, they lost time and now have an empty apartment to watch." He clapped his hands together as a child might as an expression of joy. Then he explained for Elizabeth.

Fifteen minutes was an accurate description of the time it took Nick to arrive. I stared at him, recognizing him immediately but without being able to say where I had met him or seen him. Very neat, sallow-faced, he was a toothpick of a man, with sharp cheekbones, a razor of a nose. He seemed to be startled by my presence.

With a wry smile he flicked a thumb at me. "Okay?" he asked Touse. Though it was not a guttural word, he made it guttural. Touse nodded.

He knew his way around Touse's office. He went directly to the drawer with the whiskey. After a long draught of warm whiskey and a gargling cough, he said, "Someone was up in the Stimmes apartment. The light was on. The guy down in the street . . ." He noted Elizabeth's reaction. He had pointedly ignored her presence up to that moment. "Whatsa matter? Every time Mrs. Stimmes steps out, there's been someone going into her apartment."

"This is Mrs. Stimmes," I said.

"No kidding." He didn't look surprised.

"What do you mean that someone goes into my apartment?"

"Just like I said. Not every time. Hell! The lights would go on, one room at a time, as if someone was checking every corner. I saw it." He stared at her admiringly. He winked at her.

"What about the man in the street?" asked Touse impatiently.

Nick grunted and swallowed more whiskey. "One of the lights blinked three times, and this bird takes off. He makes for a telephone down the block. Maybe five minutes pass and he pedals back up the street. He's kind of mad. He looks back up at the apartment and the lights are out. I figure it's time to play cop and give him something to think about, so I go up to him and ask him what he's up to, that I think he's loitering. I tell him, 'Move along, Mac, unless you got a reason to stay.' His name, he says is Jack Trumbull. And that's no crap. I heard of him in the business. He got no reason to stay. He was just tired, he says. 'Move, Mac,' I says, and he moves."

"Nothing very new," commented Touse.

"It's new to me," interjected Elizabeth quickly.

"Of course, of course. I'm sure it's not very comforting to you to know that someone moves through your apartment at will."

"It makes me shiver."

"We will deal with your living there in a moment," Touse said blandly. "In the meantime, I must know more about this evening."

"Well, I did as you suggested," Nick said, nodding at

Touse. "I went up to the apartment and checked it out to see what the interest was."

"How did you get in?" I asked.

He grinned. "That's my trade, getting into places where I'm not supposed to be."

"Please don't interrupt, Mr. Leeds!"

"Anyways, it was clean. So I think that whoever is interested is close by, living over, under, or on the sides. So I started making some calls on the neighbors. They're clean too. And nobody moved into the building for at least a year."

"I could have told you that," said Elizabeth.

Touse gave her a hard look, showing annoyance.

"So," continued Nick, "I went up to the roof and found an interesting thing. Without much effort someone could walk over from the next roof. Without too much effort I found an apartment in the next building that was the base of operations. No imagination! The guy who rented it was John Sayles, the guy you had picked up in Connecticut. There was someone in the apartment, but he wouldn't open the door."

With satisfaction Touse clapped his hands. "Admirable," he exclaimed. "Excellent!" He turned toward me. "Does this sound like a mild game plotted by a vegetarian dinosaur? A great deal of money was spent to prepare this plot. Much more money was spent than Mr. Stimmes had available, I would think."

"Could he have used Elizabeth's?" I asked.

Touse stared at me and slowly turned to look at her. He hadn't known that Elizabeth had money. One of the problems in dealing with people like Touse: they are so damn knowing and confident that you begin to assume they know everything. I don't think I would have mentioned learning of Elizabeth's money if the occasion hadn't presented itself to ask this question. I wonder if other people allow their decisions to be made by those who seem to be experts; how easy it is to slip into a secondary role. At least it's easy for me.

"You didn't know that Elizabeth has money of her own?" I said to Touse.

"It changes my thinking," he answered. "I think it would be wise for Nick to return to the Village and continue his watch."

The detective rubbed his chin with the back of a hand. "Hell, I can take a hint," he said. "Thanks for the chance to sit down." He shambled toward the door, halting when he reached it. "I almost forgot." He dug into his breast pocket and pulled out a worn leather wallet. He tossed it to me. "Why don't you return that to Mr. Price? I lifted it from him the night I took him home." He smiled sadly. "You remember me the night you and Price got stiff at Kup's? I thought you might."

"At the bar, right?"

"I thought you noticed me." Nick left without further ceremony. Elizabeth followed his departure with her eyes.

"An admirable detective but a very questionable person," commented Touse. And then we entered into the business of Elizabeth's funds. Her attention returned to us.

Elizabeth answered the questions simply and fully. Some of her statements were revelations. Even during the war she had lived well. No peasant life for her. Her father's money had been put in trust for her in a Swiss bank.

Touse questioned and listened. He scribbled out names she gave him. He seemed to regard her story as dubious. As she'd spell out a name, she added each time, "You'll find that I'm not lying." He'd nod. "Please check," she said. "I'm not lying, really."

The trip to France, the parachute jump described by Morgan, was not a complete fabrication. He had indeed been in France. However, he had been captured.

"I read about him in the newspaper," she said. "And I remembered that he had been a friend of my father's. Because my guardian was an important man, I asked him to do what he could to release Morgan. After he was released I took him to Spain. His health was very poor."

Eleven

I TOOK ELIZABETH HOME. SHE CLUNG TO ME, HOLDING on to my arm. We were both quiet, neither of us convinced that it was wise to return to the apartment. Touse had said that he was going to have the building kept under close surveillance. He even suggested that I stay there as an additional safeguard. "If you don't, I'll do it," he had said coldly.

"Ken will stay," Elizabeth had responded firmly.

A city can be as frightening as a dark country road when you feel the presence of a threat. I'm afraid Touse had not been reassuring. The exposure of information about Morgan had done nothing but show potential danger.

I was glad that she clung to me, for if she hadn't, I might have clung to her.

When we left the cab in front of the building, I was super-alert to sound. Our own footfalls were thumping massive noises that covered suspicious hints of other tremors of movement. I held her still to see if I could spot the source of these vague ever-present other-sounds. There was nothing but the beeps, the calls of people in the distance, the normality of the moving city.

It was almost one o'clock.

The elevator groaned and clanked; its wired emptiness was ominous as it rose through the dimly lit levels. I kissed her on the cheek and found the surface of her skin cold and damp. Her hands tightened on my arm.

We said nothing, feeling the same amorphous dread and knowing that each felt it. Our eyes met momentarily. Hers were wide, like those of children who are hungry. She shuddered; her whole body next to mine quivered when the elevator cage clinched into the stopping floor with jarring suddeness. The cage seemed loose in its place, swaying gently to the dying hum of the motor.

I pulled the gate back, pushing the floor door out so she could precede me. She held back, perhaps feeling as I did that the dim hall held the danger. I stepped out and she followed. As soon as I let the door swing back and it made contact, the motor started up and the cage began slowly descending. Both of us looked at the receding elevator. We had heard nobody downstairs who could have pushed the button.

Then a girl's voice floated up the empty space: "No, Charlie, don't do that." Elizabeth smiled frostily. We walked hesitantly to the apartment. She took a key from her purse and gave it to me. The strumming of the elevator motor was a compulsive sound. The elevator clanked and creaked as it grew nearer. I felt some relief when the key turned in the lock and the door opened.

Then I was faced with the blackness of the apartment. While I hesitated, Elizabeth leaned past me and reached into the darkness. Suddenly there was light.

There was some relief when we were both inside and the door closed behind us.

"Double-lock it," she said.

I twisted the lock until I heard the bolt slip into its place. I said that it was silly of us to worry. Morgan is dead, I explained.

"I believe in ghosts," she countered grimly. She held out her hands to me, and I took them in mine. "We must turn all the lights on." She stared hollow-eyed up the long corridor into the ominous darkness of the living room.

For that second I, too, believed in ghosts and also wanted all the lights on. I hoped that she didn't realize the depth of my own anxiety. I laughed and said, "There's nothing to worry about. The apartment is empty." I put my arm around her, and we went from room to room. The apartment was ablaze with light. To assure her of the emptiness, and also to assure myself, I flung open each closet, lunging a step into them and saying, "Boo!" We both began to laugh. I even looked under the bed.

"I know why he arranged to frighten me," she said. "He has always hated me."

"How can anyone hate you? Anyone who knows you, loves you." I was trying to keep the mood light.

She kissed me, holding me hard. She whispered in my ear, "He really did hate me."

Keeping the mood light for my sake as well as for hers

was going to be a chore. Perhaps, I thought, we could find some middle ground between fear and laughter. Laughter might not really be release, but just another face of fear.

"How about some coffee?" I asked.

"I'd rather have whiskey," she replied. "It might be nice to drink so much that we can forget everything. It might even serve as an aphrodisiac. I feel so little like it now. I'm cold. My skin is cold, and my heart is cold."

I touched her. "I feel warmth."

She slipped away from me. "I feel nothing but cold."

Conversation did not come easily. We sat near each other so that we could touch hands, even though we didn't. And we drank soberly. It might have been water, for neither of us seemed to feel an effect of the whiskey. I had to agree that there was a coldness near us, around us, within us.

At times, during the many lulls in our speaking, we found ourselves listening to the sounds of the apartment, the almost imperceptible creaks of floor boards lying dead at our feet and yet protesting.

We could hear the city, its raucous Friday night sleeplessness, but it was the outside and it was as it should have been. The sounds that gripped us were those that were probably normal in an apartment but ones that we had never listened for.

Her paleness brightened into a flush of pink. Only as I noticed this change did I realize that the whiskey was having an effect "Feeling warmer?" I asked.

"Could you really sleep with me now?"

"I really didn't ask that with an ulterior motive."

"I'd call that an interior motive." She smiled.

"Then I didn't have an interior motive." My turn to smile. I felt as though I had blushed.

"Morgan always thought I was shameless. Do you think you'd apply a word like that to me?"

"I really don't understand the word."

"Come now," she said, "if I were to ask you to do something for me, you'd think I was shameless for asking so bluntly. I might, you know. And I am shameless. If I wanted you to do it, I'd ask. I'd expect you to do it, too. Even if you thought it was a disgusting act, I'd expect you to do it." Her smile had become one of superiority. She sipped at her glass, her luminous eyes twinkling above the rim.

Suddenly her eyes widened and shifted to the brightly lit hall. "Did you hear that?" she said in a small voice.

I didn't hear anything. "What did it sound like?"

"Like someone typing." She relaxed. "I don't hear it now." Rising, she flourished her glass. "Almost empty. I'm going to have another. May I fix one for you?" I handed her my glass. I didn't rise.

She laughed and then wiggled sinuously in front of me. "A man who doesn't stand up when a lady stands should know that he will end up doing her bidding at least once that evening. She wiggled away toward the kitchen. "Do you know that I have spent most of my life in loneliness? It's a terrible thing, loneliness. Life with Morgan was lonely. I would think all day of the acts of obedience I would have him perform when he came home. I would think of terrible things for him to do. He felt that I thought of them to demean him, that I wanted him to grovel. I really didn't. I only thought of things that gave me pleasure or that I thought might give me pleasure. When you get to know me better, I'll tell you about some of the things I had him do."

Her voice faded as she ran water into the glasses.

Suddenly I heard glass shatter and then it was quiet except for the water rushing from the tap. I ran as quickly as I could to the kitchen. She was staring down in the sink at the remains of the two glasses. She looked up at me. "Look what I did," she said. "They both slipped from my hand. I thought I heard something again, but I suppose it was just the water running."

I asked her if she had cut herself. She shook her head. Opening the cabinet, I found two more glasses and prepared the drinks. "You take these. I'll be right in after I clean up the broken glass."

"Dear Ken," she said, and then she hugged me, burrowing her face into my shoulder. She took my head in her hands, studying my face; her small nose quivered as though she were a dog catching a scent. Then she kissed my lips softly, tasting my mouth. She finally released me, skipping away, snatching up the two glasses as she went. "You have a wonderful mouth, dear," she sang as though these were words to a song.

I could hear her humming in the next room. Carefully picking up the large glass pieces, I piled them aside gingerly. I didn't know where the garbage bag was kept.

"Ken?"

"Be there in a second!" I ran the tap and pushed the small slivers into the water flow to be carried away. There was something pleasant in being caught up in a kitchen chore. When I turned off the tap, I was suddenly struck by the quiet. "All finished cleaning up," I said. There was no answer. I wiped my hands on the towel clumped by the sink. I turned toward the door. "You all right?"

The complete silence held me as if it had made the air around me solid. I couldn't move. Standing there, rooted, I listened. I imagined I heard someone, and yet I didn't hear a sound. I felt someone present in the apartment. I knew it wasn't Elizabeth. Blood pounded in my head, and I was relieved that it still moved, for I was rigid with fear.

"Oh, God!" was moaned from the next room. I finally responded and rushed into the living room. Elizabeth said, "I'm going to be sick," and lurched toward the bathroom.

Following her down the hall with my eyes, I then saw that the apartment door was wide open. I was staring into the dimlit hall and saw the metal lacework of the elevator chamber. The sight of the open door instantly chilled me.

I ran after her. "Are you all right! What happened?" I could hear her retching violently. I continued down the hall and slammed the door shut, double-locking it again, thinking it was a useless gesture. "Who came in?!" I shouted. I held my hand against the door as though it might spring open.

Still no reply.

"Elizabeth!"

I hesitated to leave the door. Somewhere inside of me there must have been a primitive sense of security in keeping one hand on the door, as if I were holding back some nameless terror. I called several more times, each time more loudly.

Finally she came out of the bathroom. "Why are you shouting?" Her tone was sharp, though her lips had a small smile.

"Who was in this apartment?!"

"Don't shout."

"The door was open."

She stared dumbly at the door I was holding. She seemed to be at a loss for an explanation. "He . . ." she began and then stopped. "I," she corrected herself. "I must have opened it."

"I can't believe that."

"I needed air," she said. "I needed air desperately. I opened it for the air."

"You said 'He.' What did you start to say?"

"I never said any such thing. I think you're being very unkind to question a tipsy woman."

"You're no drunker than I am."

She started to weep as she retreated toward the living room, her small body bent, her face in her hands.

"Elizabeth," I called softly.

She turned, raised her face from her hands. "I want you to go."

"You can't mean that."

"There's no danger," she said. "That terrible squeaky-voiced lawyer is mad. I'm tired, and I want you to go. I don't want you here. I want you to go," she repeated. "Can I be any clearer than that? There isn't anything to worry about. I know that." She smiled wisely. "I don't think we're really mated, you know. You're very innocent, Ken. I know it would be better if you went. I do know best."

"You keep saying that you know this or that. Suddenly you're no longer worried about anything."

The telephone rang. Her head snapped toward the ring and then back. "Please go," she said.

"Answer the telephone."

"I want you to go." Her voice had moved from a tone of plea to that of firm command.

The telephone rang insistently. And with each ring her body tightened. I watched it coil into tension.

"Get out!" she shouted. "I don't want you here! You're a lousy lover! You understand that!" She leaped at me and pushed. Her fingers clawed at my arms.

Astonished by this attack, I gave way and backed toward the door. She was a savage animal, and each ring of the telephone made her more vicious. She ran down the hall. I was suddenly very tired. I closed my eyes. Speechless, I finally turned and let myself out. I thought I heard the lock click into place as I stood in the hall. I asked myself if I were sane; the entire evening had twisted into a charade that was totally unexpected. The telephone suddenly stopped ringing. One thought I had: somebody better in bed was calling her to make certain I was gone. I was sick with jealousy.

My helplessness was complete. I didn't know what to do. I glanced at my watch. It was after two in the morning. Groggy, I drifted away from the apartment door.

There was a somber quiet in the hall. I touched the button for the elevator. The buzz sang down the latticed hole; the cable sprung taut with a stinging whine. I had only to wait to be removed. I was being removed, I thought. Pushed, too, I added.

The moments earlier that held fear had become vaguely distant, like some nightmare vaporing away after awakening. Wakefulness was mixed with a sense of humiliation and rejection. I had allowed my defense against rejection by women to fall, and now was helpless. She didn't have to push very hard.

The street was empty. I searched it for sign of Nick or of the other myriad of detectives. There was no one at that hour. I could hear the Friday night-Saturday early morning Village catcalls and whoopdedoo down the street. A dirty light shadowed from a street lamp hung over humped-up gray cars. I looked up at Elizabeth's apartment. It was ablaze like an ocean liner on a black sea. Standing there, my head gazing upward, I felt that I had been pushed overboard and was drifting away. Hell, I thought, that's the end of Morgan Harper Stimmes and what he had left behind. I'd turn the whole damned thing over to Touse and forget it.

I lit a cigarette and began walking. I had no objective, thinking that I might retrieve my automobile from its parking lot, but I dismissed that. I found a bar that didn't look as though it would close imminently.

There's a stink to bars when they've been open too many hours. They smell as if beer has been poured on the floor and the door to the lavatory left open. Whiskey seemed appropriate and so I ordered whiskey. Halfway through my drink, I wondered if I should call Touse.

I had the telephone number of Touse's hotel scribbled on a piece of paper crammed in my pocket. "Touse?" I found it hard to call him Mr. Touse or Herman. Cigarette smoke began to fill the booth. I wished I had not smoked. My eyes burned.

His voice was faded, almost incoherent.

"This is Leeds. Elizabeth decided that we were all wet, that she didn't have anything to worry about."

This upset him, so I began to explain the details of the evening since I last saw him. As I talked, he began to say "un huh" in a regular pattern to convince me, I suppose, that he was listening, indeed hanging onto every described moment. Thus I gave him the last half-hour in Elizabeth's apartment, with all my excruciating emotional reactions.

When I had finished, he said, "You're not exactly an objective observer."

"I don't think I give a damn about Morgan's game."

"You're quite justified, I would think. But I think the game, so far, has been the laying out of rules to follow. It hasn't begun in earnest as yet. I pray it hasn't begun."

"What do you mean by that?"

"Leeds, I'm ashamed of you. Do you think a man of Mr. Stimmes' intelligence would have constructed such an elaborate series of events as a joke? Practical joking was part of his nature, but this is too much. Really much too much! I would like you to finish your drink . . ."

"How did you know where I was?"

"I can hear the noise over the telephone." He was annoyed with me. "I would like you to finish your drink and then return to Mrs. Stimmes. Wait outside the building for me. I will collect Nick from the parked car, and we will all go upstairs and see if she is still alive."

I was shocked. "Alive? Do you think she might be dead?"

"I think anything is possible. Now do as I tell you. I will see you in approximately half an hour." He hung up.

The smoke from my cigarette clogged the booth. Whirls of it curled toward the small crack in the ill-fitted door. It was noisy I thought for no reason except that I couldn't think of much.

"I don't think of other person's deaths as being of consequence," Morgan Harper Stimmes had said. His blond head rolled back while he laughed. "What do we really care about? Ourselves! Only ourselves. And why not? Admit it, Leeds, that you have risen to anger to the point of murder when you found your ego threatened. Life is only ego."

I remembered the speech, but I didn't remember when it was given. I finally pulled myself from the wooden seat in the phone booth, pushed open the door, and made my way to the bar and my drink. Half an hour was a long wait. How long would it take me to walk back? I had lost track of time after I had left Elizabeth's apartment. Ten minutes? Fifteen? I ordered another drink.

Twelve

I STOOD ON THE STEPS, EYES ALERT FOR ANY MOVEMENT in the line of parked cars. Nick was certainly well hidden if he was anywhere on the street or in any of the cars. The lights in the apartment were still bright, an array of shining windows set in the black exterior of the building. An impatience filled me; I wondered if I was late and the two had already gone upstairs. I wondered if we were justified. At the same time, there was no need for justification; I imagined Elizabeth lying dead upstairs, and was absurdly curious to discover what room she had been murdered in.

I scanned the automobiles again. Still no movement. Lighting another cigarette—when would I be able to stop smoking?—I ached with the need to have someone arrive. With that pain, I also felt weariness on the flat of my feet and exhaustion in my calves. I sat down on the step of the apartment building, leaning against the glass door.

It was almost four o'clock.

I damned Touse for being late. He wouldn't be able to find Nick either, I bet. He probably wouldn't have to since he had no intention of showing up. Grimly I considered the possibility of Touse returning to bed smug in the knowledge that he wouldn't have me to worry about, since I was snug on a stoop. Nervously I glimpsed the dial of my watch in the faint street light. Damn time for passing so slowly.

I heard a click first. Looking down the street, I saw a car door open darkly a few inches. Finally it swung wide and I saw a pair of legs emerge. It was Nick. He had been in one of the cars across the road. He stretched agonizingly, as though he had spent hours curled into a ball. He walked toward me, stiff-leggedly at first and then with a more vigorous step. He was holding something, half hidden in a hand.

He sat down next to me. His breath was a fog of whiskey. "Only way to keep warm and happy," he said, holding a pint bottle toward me. "Have a slug?"

"No, thanks."

"Got another one of those?" He flipped a thumb at the cigarette in my mouth.

"Sure." I brought out my pack and offered him one.

"Been trying to give them up. I can't do it. Got nothing else to do but smoke."

"It's a like a drug," I said in agreement.

"What are we waiting for?"

"Touse is coming."

"What the hell for?"

"He thinks she may be dead."

"No kidding." Pause. "What the hell happened? You hit her or something?"

I smiled. "She was all right when I went out. No, I didn't hit her."

"He's full of crap. Nobody went in or came out while you were gone. Where the hell did you go?"

"I went out because she told me to go. I went and had a drink and I called Touse."

"He's nuts. She's all right. There's nothing wrong up there. Makes me wonder if he's so bright." He had a broad grin, full of long teeth. His thin face was comic with this expression. He shouldn't ever smile, I thought.

"You know," he said, "this whole business is kind of oddball. Someone pays me, I do a job. But this job is kind of oddball. I work for Touse regular. He likes to know what people are doing. I never know what the hell the job is all about. I'm chasing around a lot on this one. I figure something's oddball when I start chasing after the leftovers."

"Leftovers?"

"Yeah, the body of this guy Stimmes. Oddball, like I say. Sure you don't want a drink?" The bottle danced a few inches from my face.

I shook my head.

"Used to better stuff, huh? Hell, that's what makes the world go round." He unscrewed the top and tipped the bottle to his mouth. "Aaaya!" He grinned again. "Warm."

"What happened to the other detective?"

"Figure he's around somewheres. Haven't seen him. He's keeping warm." Grin. He drank again. "Aaaya!"

"Did you see anyone go in just before I came down?"

"Hell no! Nobody. There was a couple of kids going pretty hot and heavy in the next building. Then they went, too." He ground out the butt of the cigarette that I had given him. "Got another to spare?"

I gave him another. He put it behind his ear. "I oughta buy myself a pack."

"I thought somebody might have gone up after I left." I said. "The telephone was ringing. I had an idea that she knew who was calling."

"I told you. Nobody."

I looked down at my watch.

"Forget it," he said. "He'll get here when he gets here. People do things when they do them."

"It must seem that way in your business."

"Sure, why not."

He seemed to agree to anything that he didn't want to discuss further. I didn't want to think about what was upstairs. He didn't help. What room? I wondered again.

"I don't sleep too good in the light. It don't make sense that she left the lights on and tried to sleep." He twisted and pointed up at the windows. "That one, way on the left where she sleeps, shoulda gone out. I thought about that for a while. Like when I lost the leftovers, I thought to myself that I was making a mistake in not checking. But then I thought that it takes all kinds."

"Did you make a mistake when you were following Stimmes' body?"

No smile. His eyes flashed suspiciously at me. He took the cigarette from behind his ear and lit it. "I figured I must have made a mistake. Damn thing just disappeared from the incinerator. Guy was cozy as hell. Said he had no instructions about disposal. Couldn't care less as to where it went. Son of a bitch! But it sure as hell wasn't there, and I couldn't trace how it got away. Don't go telling anybody that I made a mistake." His eyes threatened me, but I could see the nagging fear in his face that I would be justified in saying that he had indeed made a mistake.

"I don't think you were meant to be able to trace it," I said.

"It was pretty tricky," he said. "Oddball business."

We sat without talking, both smoking and staring out on the emptiness of the street. The city sounds had a new note. I could hear the garbage men clanking cans and the churning distant roar of the truck swilling the contents of the cans.

"Suppose she is dead? She won't answer the door," I said. It sounded insane.

"I got a key," he said. "Probably better to call the cops and not go barging in."

"It would be hard to explain the key," I said.

"Sure."

A cab turned down the block and stopped in front of us. Touse's ponderous shape backed out of the rear door. He waved at us and then paid the driver. He stood for a moment staring up at the lit apartment as the car drove away.

"Well," he exclaimed as he approached us, "we will check now!" He strode past us, and we followed. "Has there been anything out of the ordinary?" he asked Nick.

"Nothing."

"Were the lights all on when you left earlier? I presume the apartment all lit up is the one."

"Elizabeth and I turned them on. They're still on, as you saw."

"Odd." He swung open the elevator door and pulled back the gate and let the two of us enter. He glanced up at the structure. "I would almost rather walk up," he said with a gurgling laugh. He, too, entered.

He looked startled when the cage jolted upward. "I suppose it's safe. In any case, it's too late to worry."

"If she's alive, what are you going to say to her?"

He studied me before answering. "I will say that I'm happy to find her still alive."

He didn't smile.

It was a long ride up. I had the feeling that we were going to a funeral. Both of their faces had a masklike quality. We carried with us the pungent odor of whiskey. I wondered what Nick had done with the pint. I didn't remember his fumbling for a pocket when Touse arrived. He must have left it on the step.

After the cage docked at the top floor, rocking gently in place, the hum of the motor echoed down the long shaft. I opened the way and we walked briskly to Elizabeth's apartment.

"Well!" Touse exclaimed again, and pressed the buzzer sharply. He held it for a long moment and then twice in quick succession.

There was no sound from beyond the door.

"Have you ever considered that Morgan Harper Stimmes might still be alive?" he asked me.

"Yes. Have you?"

"Yes. But I can't support it, I'm afraid. The most difficult thing for a person to do is to disappear. It's even more difficult to fake a death."

He rang again, pushing the button for an extended period of time. I felt uneasy as I listened, thinking that we were going to awaken everyone else. Nick swiveled his head, and his eyes brushed the rest of the hallway. Touse continued to press the bell. He finally stopped. "Would you think she might have heard that if she were asleep?"

Nick lay an ear against the door. "Hell, I can't tell. I'm still hearing the ringing in my ears."

"Let me in," Touse said to Nick.

"What if she's dead? The cops won't like it if we go in illegally."

"Just open the door."

Nick pursed his lips disapprovingly. Patting his sides, he finally dug into his right pants pocket and pulled out a shower-curtain ring full of keys. He handed them to Touse, with one separated from the rest. "This will do it."

"Keys?"

"Why not? It's easier, and I had one that fit."

Touse slipped it into the lock and turned it. It caught halfway. "Jiggle it," suggested Nick. He jiggled it and it completed its turn. He turned the handle and the door opened.

It was five o'clock Saturday morning. The building janitor, a Negro woman in her late thirties, tried several keys until one finally worked. She seemed to be cowed by the presence of the policeman at her elbow. Moving swiftly aside as though she didn't want him to touch her, she spoke diffidently. "I guess that's what you want."

The policeman shoved the door open without speaking. He was a sleepy-eyed rumpled man. Nick and I followed him in. Touse hung back. He knew what to expect, for he had gone in by himself almost an hour before.

It was a grisly curiosity that shoved me forward.

"Jesus!" Nick exclaimed when he saw her.

Squatting by her body, the man in blue looked up at Nick and me. His eyes were sad, as though they had viewed some wasteful act. "Go tell my buddy downstairs that there's a woman who apparently has been murdered."

"I'll go," I said. The gorge of my stomach had risen and I could taste its bitterness. And I was about to cry. All that I could think was: why the kitchen—why was she killed in the kitchen?

I was sick in the elevator and began to bawl. I stayed downstairs. I didn't go back up. The fresh air seemed to help. After a while I controlled my sobs. I kept my head down between my knees. When I finally looked up, I found Touse sitting next to me.

"Feeling better?"

"What a horrible way to die!"

"It was probably quick, after the surprise that she was going to die."

"What was it done with?"

Touse looked curiously at me. "That'll be a problem for us."

"Why so?"

"The broken glass you picked up. A large piece of it was apparently the weapon."

"Probably with my fingerprints."

"Probably."

"Sounds like Morgan made a trap for me."

"I think the trap was secondary to the murder. However, it was certainly part of what he planned. He even had us participate in making the trap secure."

"What are you talking about?"

"Nick."

"Nick?"

"After you left, no one else entered or left the building. Nick can testify to that. What would your conclusion be?"

"That I did it."

"Inescapable."

I buried my face in my hands. It was inescapable. It was odd. I had a sense of guilt as if I had, indeed, murdered Elizabeth. In an effort to hold onto my sanity, I tried to remember every detail of my leaving, to capture the fact that Elizabeth was still alive when I left. To my consternation, I found that I remembered most clearly only that the phone was ringing. Then, suddenly, I remembered. "She double-locked the door! I heard her do it!"

"It makes no difference. It was not double-locked when I opened it. It might have made a difference had it still been double-locked. Alas! The murderer is a thinking man. The game has now begun in earnest. Mr. Morgan Harper Stimmes has made all of the rules. It is up to us to find out whom he chose for the part of the murderer. As we were all directed toward this event by Mr. Stimmes, he plucked another somewhere in this city and moved that person step by step to that moment in the kitchen."

"I have had the feeling there is no escape. No matter what I do, he seemed to have known I would do it."

Touse laid a hand on my shoulder. "We will win the game, Leeds. Never doubt that."

"I haven't got a motive."

"Don't rely on the absence of a motive. Motives are easily constructed. Most of man's actions are without motive. But we all have a genius for finding purpose in all behavior. Believe me, a motive can be found and will be found if the police believe you actually committed the murder."

"You make it sound hopeless."

"The first thing is to create doubt in the likelihood of your being the murderer." He smiled thinly at first. Then he grinned happily. "I think we can create that doubt."

The numbness of my body from lack of rest, that pain still in my stomach did not help. The emotions were washed away now. Touse may have been trying to bolster my spirit, but he had first dashed them. It was ridiculous, but I could think of no reason to doubt that I had murdered Elizabeth. Other than the fact that I became sick to my stomach when I saw her lying there with her eyes bulging and her throat a red-black scar, I couldn't develop any argument for why I couldn't have done it. That wasn't much of a fact. Why shouldn't murderers get sick? Perhaps they all do.

Thirteen

THERE WAS NOTHING TO DO. I LAY ON A BED IN A DOWNtown hotel that would be considered second rate by anyone who had seen its front lobby, and then demoted to fourth rate after seeing one of its rooms. It was also quiet and old. I followed a crack in the plaster down the wall until it disappeared behind Touse's head. He sat squashed uncomfortably in a cushiony chair with broken springs.

He was discoursing at great length on the events since I had last seen Morgan alive. Propped up on the pillows bunched behind my back and head, I nodded when he asked questions. The questions were pointless. He was simply repeating everything I had told him earlier and apparently was proving to himself that he had heard and remembered correctly. He had.

"This is boring, isn't it?" he asked after I nodded again listlessly.

"Your memory is extremely accurate," I said.

"There is nowhere else to begin. I was hoping that you might add a touch here and there."

"I don't think I left out a word in the first place."

"Apparently."

I lit another cigarette indolently.

"Would you like another drink?" he said.

"I'll get it." I twisted off the bed toward the writing table-bureau to the ice container and whiskey bottle.

"Pour me one, too, if you don't mind." His cheeks bunched to a smile. "I may as well join you. My memory seems to be intact. The creative processes are apparently slow. Only glimmerings of ideas come to me. I can't put a form to them. I wish we had the tapes," he added when I handed him his glass.

"I shouldn't think that Kelly would mind if you borrowed them. There's a transcript of them in the packing cartons." Kelly was the detective who had questioned me.

"Have you heard them all?"

"Hell no! I haven't even read all of the book notes. Stimmes' voice bothered me, I guess. I couldn't get over the feeling that he was a ghost."

"Understandable."

I was amused at myself in having a blind faith that Touse would be my savior. My mind would not leave the thought that Nick had had the opportunity to enter the apartment, and that this information was being withheld from the police. The thought nagged at me. I hadn't brought up the possibility because of Touse; he'd keep me out of trouble.

"I'm a complete blank," he said.

Perhaps I shouldn't have been amused. "To your health and mine," I toasted, raising my glass. I had made the same toast with the previous drink.

"You probably could use more sleep," he replied.

"For God's sake, wish me good health!"

He stared at me as if I were a puzzle without solution. "Good health," he finally said without emphasis.

Then there was an enormous pause, an unbearable accumulation of time during which our eyes met. I felt for the first time that he questioned my innocence, or at least had some doubts. I tore my eyes from his and looked toward the windows. It seemed ironic that the sky was so blue and I felt so gray.

"How about the apartment in the next building?" I asked.

"The police are investigating it. The confusion of material works on your behalf. It is much too complex to fix blame easily. I'm hopeful."

"I'm not." The sky was still blue. My mood was darkening. "How long are you going to stay in New York?"

"Through Monday. I'll probably return to Washington in the evening. But don't be concerned."

The telephone rang. I leaned over to answer it. "Yes?"

It was a long-distance call for Touse. I drank my drink and rose to replace it. I saw him glance at me with concern. Probably the call had something to do with me. I paused before pouring, watching him as he listened without speaking. He said, "Thank you. I'll probably see you Wednesday." He hung up. Again our eyes met.

"Did you check your mailbox when you went home to pick up the Stimmes material?"

"There was a circular in it. Most of my personal mail arrives at the college. Why?"

"My secretary just called. I have received an invitation to go to a memorial service for Morgan Harper Stimmes on Tuesday morning. I assume you should have one in your mail."

I laughed. "I don't feel exactly like memorializing Morgan at this moment."

"Neither do I. However, it will be interesting to know why he continued to plod on with his plot. He must have known that it would be anticlimactic."

"I don't think he gave a damn when he arranged for it." Touse had finally convinced me that he wasn't going to be of much help. He was enjoying Morgan's play-by-play action too much. He was hypnotized by the intellectual fun involved. I was simply a by-product. Elizabeth and I were the victims. She had suffered her end game. I was moving closer to my part. "Are you going to spend the night?" I asked.

Surprise. His melon head tilted backward. "I thought I would keep you company. Perhaps casual conversation might touch on some vital detail."

"I doubt it. You know everything I know. I don't know everything you know. After all, I haven't seen any of the stuff he wrote you."

"I don't have it with me. You know basically about everything I know."

He was being defensive. I was glad to upset him. I felt pleased that his face blushed with color. "Maybe you ought to let me go to sleep before I insult you. My mood isn't very friendly."

He pulled himself ponderously from the chair. It is remarkable how well large men carry themselves once they have their feet under them. He didn't say a word until he reached the door. "Are you going to stay in?" He twisted about on a delicate balance as if his weight were partially suspended from a balloon.

"I might go out later, if I'm up to it."

"Don't interfere with Kelly's work. It might be embarrassing for you. I think everything will go well if we are cooperative and don't interfere."

"Goodnight." I resented the use of the word "we."

It was dusk when I was preparing to go out. I found the card with the names Touse had given me the evening before. I had eaten in the hotel room while watching a newscast on television. There was no mention of Elizabeth's murder. I had expected one, with a sense of dread that I would be mentioned as the prime suspect.

As I was putting on my coat, the telephone rang.

"Ken?" Unmistakably the Touse voice.

Irritably I replied, "You woke me up."

"Sorry. I just thought of a question . . ."

"Couldn't it wait?" I bet myself that he wanted to know if I was still there.

"I thought this would be a good time, since you might be hungry and be thinking of going to a restaurant."

"What's your question?"

He was silent for a second. "Perhaps you'll have dinner with me and I could ask you then."

"Not tonight, thank you."

"Well . . ." Another pause. "Did you ask Mrs. Stimmes whether she sent the tapes to the friends of her father?"

"Who else would have sent them?"

"Assuming she wasn't lying when she told us that she had money of her own, the desire to blackmail would be gone. She wouldn't have needed money."

"It's a good question. I should have asked her, but I didn't." Perhaps Touse didn't know it, but Elizabeth had not been overly fond of her father. In my own mind I crossed off revenge as a motive for sending the tapes.

"Sure you won't join me for dinner?"

"Not tonight. Maybe tomorrow."

Once out on the street, even with night closing in on the city, I felt alive for the first time that day. The lack of restriction, the lack of Touse, gave me a freshness of spirit. I no longer felt hemmed in by my dependence on the lawyer. I was doing something to help myself.

It was a dirty tenement building where Viola Grafton and Martha Kempton lived. The brown-red facing of the building appeared to have yellowish scum creeping in rivulets down its surface. Five stories of windows were greasy, cutting off a portion of the dim bluish light inside. I remembered Elizabeth's apartment windows. They sparkled.

I double-checked the address on the card again. Then I plunged forward, as if into icy water, up the long stairs. I had never felt more hampered by my limp than I did in this determination to do something directly for myself.

The hall was in semi-darkness, lit only by a small naked bulb. It was necessary to light a match in order to see the names in their narrow line on the left of the hall. In a thick crayon print next to 3C was "Grafton-Kempton." I pushed the tiny worn black button and went to the heavy door. The door was glass surrounded by a thick black frame. The glass was covered by a dusty-brown curtain.

The doubts that my visit to the two strange women would lead to anything welled up as I waited for the entering buzz. I wondered what I would say to them if they were home.

Click, click, click came from the lock on the door. They were home. Their buzzer sounded like a pair of mating crickets. There was more light on the other side of the door. I could see on the white tile floor that someone swirled a wet grimy mop across it each day. The dry swirls were still evident, giving the floor the look of a poorly plowed field. "3C" was on the third floor, I decided.

An eye glared out at me from the crack of a narrowly open door. It moved up and down as if it were recording all of me for a file. "Yes?" a voice from beneath the eye asked. There was a gray-gold chain holding the door from the inside.

"I'm Ken Leeds. I met you on the Cape. Morgan Harper Stimmes introduced us," I said.

There was no recognition in the eye.

"I'd like to talk to you about Morgan. He's dead, you know. Now his wife is dead. This is quite important."

There was no answer.

"Morgan wanted me to invite you to his memorial ceremony." What was it called other than ceremony? Ritual? I left the word the way I first said it.

The voice: "You came to bring the invitation?"

"Yes," I said weakly.

"Give it to me." Two pudgy fingers appeared at the slit.

"Morgan wanted you both to come. There's no written invitation."

The fingers disappeared.

"I'd like to talk about Morgan, too. I know it's been a long time since we met, but Morgan left me a note with your names on it. You knew he was dead, didn't you?"

"We knew. I'm not sure we want to talk to you. We don't have very much to talk about. We don't want to get mixed up with you people."

I wondered what kind of people I was part of. The dark eye blinked nervously.

"Did you know his wife?"

"We knew her."

"Won't you let me in? It's uncomfortable out here."

The eye vanished. I could hear a mumbled conversation on the other side of the door. The eye reappeared.

"Maybe," said the voice.

I didn't know what she meant by that. I was tempted to laugh. "His wife was murdered last night," I said.

The voice gasped, and the eye was gone. There was more conversation. The door slowly closed, as if by accident. I knocked. The door opened to the same extent against the glistening chain. The low buzz of talk continued. Then, there was the eye staring at me. She didn't speak. The eye again studied me from toe to hair.

"Do they know who murdered her?"

"I'm afraid not. I was hoping you would have some information."

"Did you do it?"

"No."

The door closed. I could hear the chain being removed, so I repressed the desire to knock for attention. The door opened wide. As I had guessed, the eye and voice belonged to the stocky member of the two. The other hung back in the darkened hall, her original slimness now an angular boniness. She was a shadowy figure living in shadows. I could feel her tension in the small hall. If I were to move suddenly, I had a feeling that she would run wildly from me.

I entered hesitantly. "Miss Grafton," I said, hoping that I had chosen the right name for the one who admitted me.

"Go right in," she said. I had picked the right name.

Miss Kempton skittered in front of me. The only light was the one in the hall shining through the open door.

As I felt along the wall, I wondered if they were going to conduct the entire conversation in the dark. Then Martha Kempton struck a match in the room I was about to enter. She lit a candle.

Viola Grafton closed the door. "They turned off our electricity," she said behind me.

"Oh." The outside world was obviously "they."

"We didn't pay the stupid bill."

The skinny one used the one candle to light three more on the table. There was a strange aroma in the apartment. The candles gave out a polished oily smell. The walls were stroked with long shimmering sharp shadows.

"Do you have any money?" asked Viola.

"Yes."

"How about buying some things, like wine, so we can sit down comfortably and talk?"

I fished out my billfold. I put a ten-dollar bill on the table. Martha's pinched face seemed to be frozen by its sight. "I haven't eaten," I lied. "Let's have more than wine."

Martha lifted her head and said, "Viola?"

"You go do the shopping, honey. I'll talk to Mr. Leeds while you're out."

Fourteen

"MRS. STIMMES CAME TO SEE US SEVERAL TIMES AFTER Morgan died," Viola said. She munched on a piece of baloney, neatly turning it in her fingers, eating the edges first. Martha wasn't as delicate. She mounded two pieces into her cheeks and, with a silly smirk, chewed. "She was nice," Viola added. "She would come and sit for hours. Sometimes she wouldn't say anything. Just sit until we forgot she was here. Other times she would talk continuously about Morgan. I had the feeling she thought we had some secret we wouldn't tell her."

"Did you?"

The two exchanged glances. Martha's grin vanished. "What kind of secret?"

"Morgan had everyone keeping secrets," I said. I explained how I had been given their names and that their addresses had been given to Touse.

Viola drank her glass of milk in one continuous gulping and then poured again. "I guess we did something like that for him," she said.

"You didn't tell Elizabeth about it."

"Of course not. We had specific instructions that she shouldn't know."

"No instructions about me?"

"We knew that he thought you were a pushover. He said that he could have you do anything he wanted. He wasn't very nice about people."

My face burned with the heat of my anger. "Did you like him?"

"What's there to like?" Viola laughed. Martha stared at her, cringing slightly. Then she, too, laughed.

"We got along. He took us as we were. He'd talk a lot. I think he was crazy."

"What didn't he want his wife to know?"

Martha's eyes grew wide, reflecting the flickering light.

"We took care of his body," Viola said without hesitancy. "We made all the arrangements."

"Where are the ashes now?"

"Who said ashes?"

"I understood . . ."

"Morgan's body never got that far," Viola said. "The funeral parlor was embarrassed because it never got to make ashes of him. I had him buried."

Poor Nick, I thought. No wonder he lost the body. He was looking for ashes.

"Where is he buried?"

"On the Cape. That's where Morgan wanted it. And it wasn't hard. Morgan made all of the arrangements beforehand. The hardest part was in having the coffin moved from one funeral parlor to another one without the first one knowing."

I didn't care about Morgan's body. Maybe he thought it was a funny joke. It was the grisly notion of a sick man. I couldn't understand how the two could have gone along with it. Perhaps it was for money.

"I don't believe Elizabeth would have cared what happened to him after he died. Wasn't there something else?"

"We sent out a few things in the mail," Martha said. Her face changed abruptly from a happy helpfulness to one of fear. Viola glared at her. "What's wrong?" Martha asked in a small hesitant voice.

"For God's sake! If you don't know!" Viola had the look of a weary mother.

"What kind of things?" I asked.

"Nothing important." Viola was still glaring at her partner.

"Let me guess," I said, the truth dawning. "You sent recording tapes to some men."

"He knew," Martha said as if in defense of herself. "We weren't told not to tell him. They couldn't have been very important. I think the body was much more important." I thought she was going to cry. Viola continued to look angry.

"You told him about the body," Martha said.

"The body wasn't important."

"You told me it was."

"Who cares about a dead body?"

"It took more work."

"Work doesn't make a thing important."

"I feel like crying."

I wanted to intrude and end the bickering, but they ignored my presence so totally I felt I had no method of making them aware of me. They were caught in a sticky feminine impasse. No one had to bring problems to them; they would find them because of the sad entrapment of their lives.

"I did all the work," Martha said, her manner showing less terror.

"I had to tell you what to do. Your passivity is sickening."

What was Morgan plotting when he arranged for the tapes? So I had solved one of the mysteries, but it didn't make Elizabeth alive.

"Who did you send the tapes to?" I asked. They didn't permit me entrance to their conversation until I repeated my question and raised my voice.

Martha swung her head toward me. She seemed to be stunned for a moment that I was there. The candlelight made her face a comic mask with deep fluctuating shadows. She looked imploringly at Viola, as if to call her attention to the sudden appearance of a stranger.

"Christ, I don't remember," said Viola. "Just names."

"The same names, both times," added Martha. Her eyes flashed defiance at Viola.

"There you go again," said Viola disgustedly, "giving more information than you were asked for. Why the hell don't you leave the talking to me!"

"Both times?" I asked, surprised.

"Maybe he ought to know. Mrs. Stimmes is dead," Martha said.

"Morgan said it was a secret," Viola said. "He paid so it would be a secret."

"Do you know what the two tapes said?" I asked.

"Who the hell listened?" Viola said.

I looked at Martha. She shook her head. "You really didn't know?" I asked.

"Who the hell can afford a tape recorder?" Viola said.

"Morgan didn't tell you?"

"He didn't tell us anything. He paid bills when there was no other way to pay bills," Viola said.

Martha looked pained.

"Why shouldn't he know?" Viola said to her. "He might as well know. Embarrassed, honey?"

Martha burst into tears and dashed like a gazelle from the table into a dark room.

"You pleased now?" Viola stared at me accusingly.

"I'd think you'd both be more sensitive about other things than owing money."

One of the candle nubs in the middle of the table burned its last and flared to a high flame before sputtering into blackness. We both watched it.

"Damn," she said without emphasis. "That's the way the money goes. You know, we blew the last ten dollars Morgan gave us by going to the Radio City Music Hall and buying two huge bags of popcorn. Like a stinking candle!"

I took a ten-dollar bill from my wallet and placed it on the table. "Won't help much, I'm afraid," I said. Then I rose and began to go.

"Wait a minute."

I turned to see the chunky figure hunched over the bill, apparently studying it. She snapped it as if to see if it would tear apart. "You don't have to do this."

"I know. I thought you might want to go back to Radio City Music Hall."

"Not funny."

"I guess it's not. What else do you want me to say?"

"It's pretty decent."

"Thanks for the information." I was about to go again.

"I told you to wait a minute."

"I know what you told me. I don't think there's any more to talk about."

"Martha!" she called. There was no reply. "Martha!"

The pale and thin Martha reappeared at the doorway. She didn't commit herself to forward motion; there was more evidence that she would return to the darkness, her figure coiled to react.

"You can give him the names, dearie."

Martha stood still.

"I mean it. You can give him the names. It's all right."

Martha still didn't move. Finally, hesitantly, she crossed to the table. "One of the candles is gone," she noted in a whisper of a voice. Viola paid no attention. Martha picked up one of the longer candles, and carrying it before her, walked with increasing dignity into another dark room, a loop of dim light preceding her.

"She's a nice girl," Viola said. "But it's a crummy life we got. You know what I mean. I suppose it's my fault. I take the blame."

I don't think she was talking to me. She was just talking

because someone was present who didn't care what she said.

"Hell, she didn't have much before I found her. Guess I can't blame myself." Suddenly the stockiness whirled around toward me. "You know, that sonuvabitch Morgan was a sonuvabitch! No kidding! If I didn't know he was dead, I'd swear he killed his wife. He was crazy."

"You sure he's dead?"

"I saw that sonuvabitch laid out. And he was cold. He was a mess. He was dead, all right."

"I sometimes think of him as still alive."

"You know what that crazy sonuvabitch once said. He said some scientist was one day gonna dig him up and put his bones in the Smithsonian. What the hell do you think he meant by that?"

I didn't answer. I'm not sure she wanted one.

The circle of light bloomed from the blackness and Martha reappeared. She held an index card.

Fifteen

I SLEPT POORLY, EVEN THOUGH I FELT A DESPERATE need for sleep. I didn't know what to do with the information I had received. I thrashed about on the soft bed.

The phone rang. The room was washed with morning light.

"I'm downstairs and coming up. Thought I'd warn you first in case you were still asleep," Touse said.

"I was asleep finally."

"It's good you're awake now, then." It was a humorless remark.

I bolted for the bathroom to prepare myself. I was in the middle of shaving when I heard a knock at the door. "Damn it, Touse," I greeted him on opening the door, "it's Sunday morning. I always sleep late on Sundays."

He paid no attention. "While you finish shaving, I'll order some breakfast."

When I faced him. I felt somewhat better, more prepared for his questions. I knew he would have questions.

"Tuck your shirt in," he said.

I smiled and did as he said.

"What did you do last evening?"

"You telephoned."

"No, I didn't. I'll be fair, though you are not being fair with me. Although Nick is no longer participating, you are still being followed."

"I wasn't being a very bad boy," I said. "I didn't see any harm in seeing Miss Grafton and Miss Kempton. It turned out to be informative."

"I visited them already." There was a look of pride on his face, a tilt to his nose that told me he considered my evening a waste of time.

"I didn't learn that," I said. His lips bowed into a superior smile. "I suppose they told you about the body."

"Of course."

There didn't seem to be any point in withholding my information. I took the card that Martha had given me from the top of the television set and handed it to him.

"These are the three people who received the tapes. They each got two tapes. Miss Grafton and Miss Kempton sent them."

"Two tapes?"

"So they said."

"I knew about one."

"I didn't know about the second one either, not until last night."

"Hmmm."

"That's an understatement."

"Did they listen to both of them."

"They didn't listen to either of them."

Breakfast arrived. A tap-tap at the door, and a dour man in a wrinkled uniform pushed a cart into the room. Touse dug out of his pocket a crumpled mass of bills, giving one to the man. "Ah," Touse said, paying no further attenion to the thanks he received. He lifted the cover off each dish, whiffing at the rising steam. "Ah," he said again.

My impresssion was that he liked food, but I was wrong. He dipped an English muffin into the yellow of his fried egg, took one bite. He drank his orange juice and then poured his coffee. He was done except for drinking his coffee, which he kept black.

I was starved, devouring two eggs completely, a rasher of bacon, toast, juice. "Want the rest of your muffins?"

"You may have them."

And muffins. Then coffee, with sugar and cream.

"Not hungry?" I asked.

"I'm very quickly satisfied." He smiled. "I don't know why I gain weight. It has always been thus." He settled himself in the straight chair as if he were making a place for his body in a nest. "Do you have a cigarette?"

I handed him my pack.

"An indulgence with my coffee," he explained. He held it between his thumb and next three fingers as if he were unaccustomed to smoking. I lit it for him. "Do you have a good view?" he asked.

"The street and tall buildings," I answered.

"Too bad."

"You're not very good at casual conversation."

He looked pained. "I'm digesting breakfast. Also digesting your information."

"You make a lot of money at law?"

"I think so. I always have money left over at the end of the year. However, I have very few personal expenses so that may not be a good criterion. Why do you ask?"

"I just wanted to know if you could understand Morgan's desire for money. He couldn't make a living any longer at his profession, if you call it a profession. I'm beginning to think that Morgan's relationship to money is important."

He hummed to himself briefly, looking first at the card of names I had given him and then at me. "These are very important men," he noted. "They were all, I assume, associated with Mrs. Stimmes' father."

"I made the same assumption."

"We must tell this to Kelly."

"What the hell for?" I didn't understand Touse. I had thought that Touse would join me; perhaps we might go see the three men, open up another avenue of investigation.

He clucked disapprovingly and wagged a finger at me. There was something of the Buddha about him, that overwhelming inscrutable knowingness. "Detective Kelly should be told about this. Any time he thinks we are withholding information, he'll begin wondering about the extent of it that we're keeping to ourselves." He smiled toothily. I thought he was going to laugh, but he didn't. "He is coming over this morning."

"Here?"

"Here. He said he would come after attending Mass. I invited him."

He puffed at his cigarette hastily, taking the burning edge close to his fingers. Then he dropped it into the ash tray, where it continued to smoke. He paid it no attention, letting it curl in gray blue coils between us.

"I don't understand why you invited him," I said. "What's to be gained?"

"Friendship."

"He seems like a nice enough guy, but I'd rather he stayed where he is and I stay where I am."

"That 'nice enough guy' is at the moment a guy who can influence the rest of your life. Be friendly. Be nice. Be kind."

I put out my cigarette on top of his smoldering one, ending its smoke. There wasn't much I could say. I would be friendly, nice, and kind. "You know," I said, "the big mistake I made was when I went and had a drink with Morgan Harper Stimmes in the beginning."

Kelly, John was a personable man. There are men like John Kelly that I think belong inverted as Kelly, John. He looked as though he had nothing to do but drop by for a casual visit. A neatly polished man, with a crisp press in his trousers, a sharp part in his black hair, a boyish smile on his face, he was competely at home. He looked as if he belonged on an IBM card, but he didn't act like it.

There was still coffee in the pot. He helped himself, pouring it into a glass, drinking it lukewarm and black.

One thing about Kelly began to bother me. No matter how critical a situation, he smiled as if he saw humor where everyone else saw an apparently superficial and passing tragedy. He gave me a sense of guilt for not being perceptive enough to see the deeper and funnier truth. It was infectious. Even Touse began to smile.

"That's sure a lot of material you brought me," Kelly said as he twisted a chair about so that he straddled it backwards, leaning on its support. He laughed. "Sure you're not trying to get it indexed without paying?"

"That's the only reason I gave it all to you," I said. "It's for a book, you know."

Gloom crossed Touse's face, a squashed rumple of distaste.

"I thought so." Kelly grinned.

"There's an awful bunch of dull stuff. I never did finish reading all of it. As a matter of fact, I haven't read much of it. I'd always get caught looking for things that Morgan wrote that didn't have much to do with the book," I added.

He grinned again, a white sheen of good nature and good-guyism. Touse half-heartedly joined him with several almost soundless hrumphs of laughs.

"Found out something last night that might help you," I said. "He'll tell you about it."

Touse looked startled at my sudden introduction of the material he said he was going to pass on to Kelly. He glared at me. Then he turned his attention to Kelly. "A tragic death. Mrs. Stimmes was a young woman with great beauty and great wealth, I believe," he began.

There was a speech in him that he was going to give before he did anything else. I wandered to the window and stared down at the street, watching the Sunday traffic sluggishly move at Sunday pace.

In his little boy's voice, Touse continued. I recognized some of the statements as those he had already made to Kelly yesterday. I wondered if I should show interest in order to be friendly, nice, and kind. I continued to stare out of the window.

I was suddenly aware that Touse had slipped from his speech to the Grafton-Kempton disposal of Morgan's body and the mailing of the tapes.

"As you can see, there are some very complex problems." Touse concluded.

"No question about there being planning," Kelly said. "What do you say Ken? We got a real mastermind going on this one." His eyes were cold and blue. I had a feeling that he was fitting me with the label of mastermind. "You're a college professor, aren't you?"

"That doesn't amount to much when it's a comparatively new college, even if it's fairly big now." I felt I had to play down his image of me as a possible master planner.

"Can't get over how all of you ended up doing everything a dead guy wanted you to do." He slapped the edge of the table good-naturedly. "I was telling my wife about it last night. She came up with a theory."

Touse leaned forward in anticipation.

"My wife bet me that you didn't do it."

I was iced by quick panic. Had Kelly taken the opposite side of that bet? I didn't want to stay in the same room with him. I couldn't stand staring at his shining teeth. I looked to Touse for aid. He was no help. "I hope she wins," I said.

Kelly's eyes finally left me, wandering to Touse. "Fat chance she has. She's never been right. She always tells me that this time she's right. Fat chance, I tell her. Good sweet woman, but she don't know beans about people who do things like slitting someone's throat." Kelly slapped the table for emphasis. "Interesting fact," he said, his eyes and teeth glittering at me, "your fingerprints are all over the piece of glass that was used."

I explained for the second time how I had picked up the broken pieces of the drinking glass. Again he didn't look impressed.

"If I wasn't the kind of a guy I am, I could wrap this thing up and say you did it." The glittering never ceased. "I like to study," he continued. "When I go home at night, I study. Most guys wrap themselves around a bottle of beer and a TV set. Not me. I study things. Tell you the truth, I'm getting a boot out of the stuff you brought over. I'm beginning to study this guy Stimmes. I got a book of his out of the library and was studying it last night. He had a gift. Made me feel he was some sort of superman. Really got it across. I went to the office this morning before Mass just to read some of the things he wrote. I listened to a tape." His eyes pierced me. I was a butterfly being attached to a card. "I can't get over a smart guy like you. Didn't you know he was a phony?"

"I guess I didn't."

"Phony as a three-dollar bill." He nodded knowingly toward me and then at Touse. "But that's not helping us, is it? So maybe I ought to listen for a while and let you guys talk." And he was quiet, his hands urging us to speak—beckoning as though he were conducting music.

As if to break the awkward silence, Touse began repeating his theory that Morgan had planned for someone to kill Elizabeth, had picked the murderer and motivated the crime. I wondered why Touse had invited Kelly to my room; he seemed ill prepared for the visit. As Touse continued, Kelly nodded and smiled encouragement.

Touse ended by thrusting the card with the three names in front of Kelly. "Here are three men who felt they were being threatened. One of them might have done it."

Kelly took the card and stared at the names. "You're kidding," he said. "There's not one of them less than seventy years old." He clapped his hands together. "Old men don't go around murdering young women. And rich old men don't stand trial for murder, believe you me! And these three are rich old men!"

"Even if they were being threatened with exposure of an enormous financial scandal?" I asked.

"How big is enormous?"

"I don't put anything past Morgan Harper Stimmes! I think he knew that one of those three was capable of a murder or at least of hiring a killer! And he pushed hard to force him to do it! I agree with Touse!"

"How many patsys does a guy get in a lifetime? He already had you!" Kelly shouted back at me. He stretched his long legs in front of him, nervously pinching the crease of his pants. He raised his eyes from the table to look at me. His face was sad. "Sometimes it just comes out. Sorry. No offense. I just don't see it. You two will have to try another idea. That one doesn't hit me right. Try me along the line of some prowler creeping down the fire escape and surprising her?"

"I didn't even know there was a fire escape," I said morosely.

"Sure you knew there was a fire escape. Every building has to have a fire escape. It was down the back of the apartment."

"Is that the theory you're going on?"

"I didn't say I thought it was possible." His lips arched into contented superiority. "I wouldn't believe it if you told me that you knew it happened that way. It didn't. There's a quarter-inch of New York soot on the fire escape that hasn't been disturbed for at least a week. But if you want to know something funny: someone used to go in and out of that window a lot."

"What window?"

"The room where the books are. I guess it's where Stimmes worked." He folded his hands in front of him as if in prayer. "An interesting picture comes to mind of a man slipping away from his wife during the night. He apparently even oiled the ladder down from the fire escape. Big guy, was he?"

"Big guy," I confirmed. I, too, pictured him. I could see him furtively toeing his way down the metal stairs. It was disturbing, for I had just about completed a new image of Stimmes. He was no longer the lion; he was a jackal. If his own concept of being a dinosaur had bearing, he was now the lumbering predecessor of the jackal. He was a creature of the dark that ate offal.

"I'm a cynic," Kelly said. "You show me a great man and give me a few days and I'll tell you what he's got hidden. I like guys like you. Fumbling normal guys who make obvious mistakes. Just like me—confused miserable guys trying to be a little better." He suddenly roared with gasping laughs. "Listen to me! Who the hell gives a damn what I think!"

Though apprehensive about Kelly, frightened by him, I found I liked him. I give a damn, I thought.

"What did that accomplish?" I asked Touse after Kelly had left.

"I don't know," he answered. "I hope something."

"You weren't much help."

"That's being candid."

"Kelly made it clear that I make a good strong suspect.

He's betting I did it. It would be hell to go to the electric chair just because I was polite."

He giggled.

"It's not funny."

"I've often wondered why some of my clients become abusive. I think you've answered my question. They can't stand being polite when it looks as if I can't help them. When did you lose your trust in me?"

It didn't seem possible to me that he would begin to analyze my emotions when that was the last thing that would do me any good. I just stared at him helplessly.

Sixteen

ALTHOUGH I KNEW THAT BOTH TOUSE AND KELLY WOULD disapprove, I decided that there might be something to gain if I talked to the three men who had once been friends of Claude Wester.

On the first two men, I had no luck. I wasn't able to reach beyond a secretary who took my name and number. In desperation, I told the third secretary that my name was Morgan Harper Stimmes.

"You bastard, I should have know you were still alive! I should have known Claude's daughter couldn't have done this alone!" Bixey Pratt let loose in a torrent. There was no culture in his voice. The pretense of society was stripped down to a rasping irritated anger. There was no sign of an old man; he sounded like a street mongrel of fourteen. I let him talk.

"I've told them to go ahead with the friggin' book and even the *View* piece. What the hell do you want from us? Claude was a bastard. He took most of it. That's the way he wanted it. After all these friggin' years . . ." I could hear him breathing heavily during the sudden pause. "Morgan?" The rush of words was over, I decided. His initial reaction had flooded out; now he questioned. It was time to tell him.

"I'm not Morgan. I'm Ken Leeds."

"You sonuvabitch!" He hung up.

The image of Elizabeth lying on the kitchen floor filled my mind. I grabbed my coat and left the room. I was going to see Pratt in person. He had said enough to give me evidence that I might be right about the three old men.

It's a terrible part of the city, worse than the penny-arcadism of midtown. Property is clearly more valuable than people on Wall Street; the buildings barely leave enough room for people to move among them.

Any hesitance I had about meeting Bixey Pratt face to face vanished after his secretary returned from his office to say that he was free and waiting for me.

It was a big office. If size was a measure of a man's stature, Pratt's measure was calculated in yards, not feet. There was an alcove to the right, cut off the main section by a waist-high bookcase. I bet myself that the other side, back-to-back, was a refrigerator, bar, you-name-it convenience. On one wall was an enlarged photograph of a nighttime view of the New York skyline. I recalled Morgan's first interview tape. He had made a casual reference to the beauty of just such a photograph. I was standing in the office of the man Morgan was going to crucify.

He was unctuous. A short skinny man, with a dimpled prominent chin, fluffed-up white hair, he sprang from behind his desk. "Sorry about the call being cut off," he said. His skin was unwrinkled. He might have been a prematurely white-haired fifty. He had a firm grip.

"If I had known where you called from, I would have called you back."

"I'm sorry about using Morgan's name."

He began to override my apology as soon as I started. "A mistake of judgment, no more."

What other kind of mistake was there? I wondered.

"What can I do for you, young man?"

I explained that it was up to me to find someone to complete Morgan's book.

He was fiddling with a console of buttons in a small white box near his phone. "And what can I do?"

"I don't like to allude to your words on the phone, but it sounded as though you thought I was about to blackmail you."

His finger touched a button. "I don't have any interest in Claude Wester or his difficulties over the Vanishing Indian." His fingers played delicately over the buttons.

"You recording our conversation?" I asked.

His rosy skin darkened. I could sense the violence in this man. What held him to his chair? He slumped back after tensing forward. "Ours is a private conversation, young man. That's a rudeness."

"I'm not above being rude at the moment. Someone murdered Morgan's wife. I thought it might be you." I smiled. That was blunt. I expected he would throw me out.

The blood drained from his face. He tugged his hands

to his chest as though they had been too close to the fire. "Jesus!" he finally said. I knew he wasn't going to throw me out. He looked genuinely shocked.

"Did you think she was the one sending you the tapes?"

"I don't know what you're talking about." If his voice usually reflected emotion, he was showing none.

"I know you received two tapes. I found out the other night who sent them. You were one of three who received them. George Teagarten came to see me after the first one apparently was put in the mail."

"I still don't understand why you're interested." He had remarkably little expression in his eyes. They were two gray pebbles.

"I think you or one of your friends murdered her."

"Neither I nor my friends murder people," he snapped.

There was a small fire in the pebbles. "At least answer my questions."

"Young man, your questions don't deserve answers. Why don't you do as Morgan suggested? Find someone to complete the book on Claude and go back to teaching school. Whatever happened to Mrs. Stimmes is of no concern to you or to me. I'd suggest you forget it and go home."

"I'm trying to do you a favor. Morgan's wife didn't send you the tapes. Someone else did."

The pebbles stared at me. I watched the heat behind them die out. My words were finally beginning to sink in.

"Tapes?" he said.

"Tapes," I repeated. "Let's not forget the conversation we had on the phone this morning. You may think you're kidding me and think I'll forget it, but believe me, I have the words imprinted on my mind."

"It's not necessary to bring it up. I know what I said." There was annoyance in his voice. He rubbed a finger in the dimple of his chin.

"I'd like to hear the second tape. I've heard the first." At once I was sure I shouldn't have admitted ignorance of the second tape's contents. "I'll find out," I said lamely. "Then we'll talk again!"

He smiled with a curve of tight lips. They reminded me of a moon sliver. There was a coldness in his pleasure. "I don't think we'll talk again," he said.

My anger had not died down by the time I arrived back at my hotel. Die down? It increased as I went over every frustrating scrap of conversation. I damned myself for stupidity and I damned him generally. Perhaps it was irrational because of the anger, but I was positive I had looked into the eyes of a murderer. In my mind I saw Elizabeth's kitchen and I saw him stealthily creep up behind her and draw the piece of glass across her throat. My agitation was as deep as when I had seen her body. I'm helpless, I thought. There's nothing I can do. My anger was bordered with fear.

I turned the key in my room's door lock. I instantly knew something was wrong. Pitter-patter was the sound in the room. Also an aroma of a strong tobacco wafted from the partially opened door. I checked my key against the door number. They matched. I was positive I was on the right floor.

I swung the door the rest of the way. Not knowing what to expect, my sense of fear widened. I saw an old man seated in a wheelchair, with a blond tan-faced youth behind him holding onto the chair's handles. The old man was covered with a red and black checked robe. His face was wrinkled with fat folds of plaster-white skin. His eyes looked as startled as mine must have been. I again wondered if I had blundered into the wrong room.

"You're in the right room," the youth said. "Mr. Seed would like to talk to you. I brought him up." He ducked his head at me and then leaned over the old man. "I'll be outside, Mr. Seed." He stepped by the wheelchair, winked at me, and passed me. He closed the door behind him.

Mr. Seed was Lawrence Seed, one of the old men on my list.

"I'm sorry," he said, "for seeing you under these circumstances." He weaved a hand shakily through the air. The hand held a cigar. An ash dropped from it to the floor. "I wanted our meeting to be secret." There was no expression on his face. His voice was dead and monotonal, lacking even emphasis between loud and soft.

"I called you this morning, but your secretary wouldn't let me talk to you."

"I know, I know," he said. "I managed to find you, in any case. I must talk to you, if you'll consent to listen." His voice for the first time began to drop to a conspiratorial whisper. I bent forward to listen, finally moving to him and sitting in a chair next to him.

"A terrible thing has been done," he said. "I do not condone the murder of a young woman so that age might be preserved in honor. We took millions, son. We took millions. It just happened. We didn't even plan it. It was there and we took it. It was like being in a vineyard when all the grapes were ripe. We gathered grapes. There was no justification. We didn't need the money. Now a young woman has been killed. I've been sitting in this wheelchair for fifteen years. There's no pleasure left. Just life. Now a young woman has been murdered."

I never had occasion before or since to listen to a man confess a crime. However, I had lost interest in his crime. Perhaps I should have felt some desire for retribution.

"How did you know that Mrs. Stimmes had been murdered?" I asked.

"I knew she would be killed. I knew one of us would kill her."

"How did you know?"

"To protect old men. The oldest struggle in the world is between age and youth. Age hangs on. Age will murder to prolong life-with-honor for a single minute. I have no more money. I'm wheeled into an office each day and I watch television and smoke cigars. My sons own everything. They won. I lost. But I didn't know about the struggle until it was over. They want to keep me at home, but I won't let them do that. I want them to see me, to know what they did to me. They hate me and I hate them. My only friend is that boy outside, because he will take me anywhere I want to go."

His mind had wandered. I now knew what the companion's wink had meant. Was any of the conversation rational? I wondered.

"Who do you think killed Mrs. Stimmes?" I asked desperately.

"Age kills youth," he answered. "I've seen young men grapple with the old until the death. My sons. They've stripped me of everything but life. All I can do is outlive them. I'll watch their children do the same thing to them, and I'll laugh."

He never smoked his cigar. His palsied hand weaved it quiveringly during his moments of excitement. He must have been in the room for a long time. I could see that he had been near the window, for a scatter of ashes was there.

"Did you receive the second tape?"

He was silent, as though desperately trying to understand me. The fat flesh moved into new folds with the effort.

"Did you receive any tapes?" Then I shouted, "Which one of you killed her?"

Blankness. "My sons . . ." He had lost the thread of his thought. "I become tired easily," he finally said. As though that were his cue, his head nodded to the side. His eyes closed under a flab of fat. At first I thought he had died on me, but he continued to breathe deeply and noisily. His hand with the cigar hung limply over the side of the wheelchair. I leaned forward and removed the cigar.

I went to the door and motioned to the young man.

"Pops is out, huh? I was surprised he lasted this long. Must have really wanted to tell you something."

I gave him the cigar, which he stuck in his mouth.

"He probably won't remember a thing about this. Don't tell his sons. They don't like me taking him around unless they know. Pops was pretty set on their not knowing. We can keep a secret, huh?"

"I'll keep it a secret."

The phone rang that afternoon. I was stretched out on the bed in a tense wakefulness.

It was Kelly. He was angry. "For my sake, leave Alexander Treat alone." At first the name didn't register. "He's sore as hell. Called the Mayor and I don't know who else. Claims he's afraid you're some kind of extortionist."

"Who?"

"You been asleep? You sound groggy."

"Alexander what?"

"Treat."

"The last of my old men."

"What do you mean, the last of your old men?"

I explained the calls I had made and the two visits. He was silent. I could hear him breathing heavily. Then he said, "Protect me from guys like you."

"Doesn't it sound as if one of them killed her?"

"Just suppose you're unlucky enough to accuse the right guy. Bang, you're dead." His laughter rose as if he had made an extremely funny joke. "I suppose you don't have anything to lose," he added. "If you killed her, you're going to end up dead anyway."

Seventeen

IT WAS ELEVEN O'CLOCK WHEN SOMEONE KNOCKED ON THE door. I had already heard a news report on Elizabeth's murder and was about to watch the news to see if any further developments had been released.

I turned the set off and went to the door.

"I took a chance that you'd be in and came without calling." Touse's ponderous form loomed expectantly in. There was no way of avoiding him. He lugged in a large satchel-like object. "Ready for the ceremony tomorrow?" he asked as he brushed by me.

"I didn't receive my invitation yet," I said, closing the door.

"I have a surprise for you," Touse said. He laid the gray case between his feet and began unlatching it. I recognized it finally as a tape recorder. As he opened it, his head bounced up and swiveled while he glanced quickly about. "Not interrupting anything?"

"Nothing going on. Spent a quiet day."

"Not entirely quiet. Kelly told me about some of your day." He bowed his head again down to the machine. "One of the police found an interesting thing—a tape—hidden in the Stimmes apartment behind a combination English-Latin copy of Caesar's Gallic Wars. Trot, trot. Understand?"

"No."

"Goodness. Don't you remember that cryptic note that you found in a carton about trot, trot. The Game. I believe this is what Morgan Stimmes meant, because it was hidden behind a Latin trot."

I remembered. However, I had dismissed it because it didn't seem to make sense. "How did you get it?"

"Kelly allowed me to make a copy of it." He arched his

eyebrows. "I wish it made more sense. The only thing I'm hopeful about"—he smiled as if hopefulness was highly unlikely—"is that there is sense to be made from this tape. It's a puzzle. Having learned to respect your intellect and ability . . ."

"Don't butter me up, Touse."

He grinned. "Now for a plug." He glanced about and moved the recorder to the bed. He pulled the bed from the wall and removed the prongs of the bed lamp from its socket, inserting the one from the player. He turned the set on, warming it. The tape had already been placed for operation.

I waited. He hesitated before turning the control. He stared at it; his hand hovered above it. Then he put his hand on the bed instead. He studied me questioningly.

"What's the problem?"

"How much affection did you have for Mrs. Stimmes? Would it disturb you if you heard her voice again?"

"I don't know. That probably answers both of your questions. Is her voice on the tape?"

"Yes."

"Play it. Like most memories of a person, I find her image is receding from my mind. Her voice might be disturbing. Let's chance it. I learned long ago that there's not much gained by trying to keep someone alive in your mind. That sounds pretty cold, doesn't it? I don't mean it that way."

"I know what you mean." His hand fell to the knob and the tape began to play.

"This is silly, Morgan. I really don't understand you. Why should I want to hear my voice?" Her voice sounded clear but distant.

"Don't question me, honey. I just want you to read this bit of nonsense. It's not objectionable." His was closer. It was a clear voice without a murmur of what I remembered in our last conversations.

"May I read it first?"

"By all means."

"You want me to read all of this aloud?"

"Every bit of it." He was obviously irritated.

"I can think of something much more pleasant."

"Just read the damn thing! Tape costs money. I have it running now."

"Why not turn it off?"

"I don't want to."

"You're a miserable person."

"So you've told me. Now read it!"

"All right!" Elizabeth coughed. *"I cannot stand because I have one foot shorter than the other."* She paused. "I hope you're not going to let that nice Mr. Leeds hear this."

"I doubt if Leeds will ever hear it."

"Turn it off!" I said.

Touse opened his eyes, glanced at me, leaned over, and twisted the dial.

"She was telling the truth. His voice, when I talked with him during those last days, was faked. He could speak perfectly normally."

"I don't understand."

"I met her after he was using that ghastly whisper."

"Unimportant." He turned the tape on.

"It takes me a terribly long time to move along on my belly to arrive at that place where I am going." Pause. "Really, Morgan!"

"Read it, damn it, read it!"

"You're awful!"

"I know. Just continue."

"I no longer have to crawl when my father once decided to roll me about in a wagon. He says that this will not be so that I am not dishonored but rather so that I will be able to live in honor." Pause. "What's this for? It doesn't make sense."

"I told you it was nonsense."

"You still haven't told me what it's for."

"A game, darling. We are playing our part now. The others will play long after you and I are gone. I'm leaving this for posterity, so that coming generations will puzzle over this strange society of ours."

"You're mad."

"True. Read."

"My husband agrees with my father's idea, though he continued to believe that I was being too protected and that the legal authorities might object while it continued. The description, a better one of a female than a male, is implicating of so much more, though you might find that it is a vanishing one. Is that meant to be sexy?"

"Is that all you think about?"

"I thought there might be something sensible when you had a male and female in it." She snickered. "In that strange repressed life of yours you even made an error in spelling."

"I never . . ."

"There." Again she laughed. "You even made it on the wrong one. Female is never, my husband, treated or spelled as you do."

Touse stopped the tape. "F-E-M-A-I-L," he spelled.

"I think she gave us the clue to the entire business without realizing it," I said.

His eyebrows arched.

"I'll bet he put her words onto another tape after rearranging them. Maybe not all of them. If I'm right, one of the words is 'mail'—M-A-I-L. And he slipped and spelled it as the word he was thinking of."

"I agree." Touse said. "Possibly an extortion request."

"The three old men." Extortion might be too simple. Morgan might try for some deeper motivation. "The mention of honor and dishonor might be something more direct, probably better than money to motivate the three old men. If Morgan was setting Elizabeth up for murder, he might be afraid they would pay off instead. Ruin the whole business."

Touse nodded in agreement. He started the tape again.

"I'll never understand why you wanted to marry me."

"I promised your father."

"I should have known better."

"You'll be rid of me soon."

"I don't want to be rid of you. I've loved you deeply but I don't understand why you treat me this way. I'm not a brutish animal and neither are you."

(There was a clicking sound, and then the voices continued.)

"Why did you turn it off and then on again?"

"There's no need for posterity to delve into our sex lives." He laughed wildly. "Mustn't corrupt humanity just because it is corruptible. Preserve its innocence. Now if you'll continue reading, Elizabeth, we can be finished and then take care of your desires."

"To live with splendid and Indian views of beauty is all

that really matters. To have lived too long without it is, in the swindle of the time in which we live, a poor thing. In a wheeled cart, we cannot escape, you cannot escape, none of us can escape the knowledge that this is true. But first you must know the joys of the cart. Believe me, I know, for I kept very good records. Hmm, I suppose even nonsense sometimes makes sense. I wish I knew what some of your symbols meant. It may be that I'm beginning to understand your madness. I think I'm beginning to understand this."

Morgan roared with laughter.

"Immediately after the service of the wheeled cart, as it moves me . . . I'm sorry . . . *after it moves me, I find that copies and the originals might be obtained of my impressions on many papers, while you sit with your many reputations, are available for a fuller understanding of life. Of how this came about and a most true version, you must ask someone else. My father doesn't understand. My husband doesn't understand.* Why are you smiling? That's absolutely the most evil smile I have ever seen, Morgan."

"That's the end," Touse said, turning the machine off.

Eighteen

I WAS AWAKE. THE NOISE OF AN EARLY MORNING CAR zoomed distantly, dying in the flat and obscure sound of city silence. The darkness of my room was filtered with slatted venetian-blind light from outside street lamps and blinking neon signs. I listened. There was a difference. I couldn't judge what it was I heard, but I knew that I had a reason to be awake.

Then I saw the source of the faint tickling of a noise, like that of an insect moving its armored body. The door eased open an inch. A narrow border of white light poured over the edges of the door, painting itself along the wall.

I caught my breath. Hesitant to move, I felt the desire to pull my covers up as if they would protect me. It was more than hesitance; it was fear. It suddenly seemed very logical that someone would want to kill me. Staying in bed was not logical.

I bolted from the bed, toward the door. I had no desire to grapple with the intruder, just a strong wish to have the strongest possible position. With a hobble and a leap, I threw my weight against the door. It slammed. I turned the double lock. There was a gasp of surprise on the other side. Then I heard someone running.

"Dear God!" I wailed. I was torn between a desire to open the door again to see who my visitor was and one to stay safe and alive. "Dear God!" I repeated. "Someone doesn't like my questions." I also knew that I was not going to be able to fall asleep again. I didn't want to sleep.

I ran to the telephone. I reported that someone had tried to break into my room. The desk clerk seemed unconcerned and asked me if I wanted to speak with the manager. I told him that he could speak with the manager and that if the manager was interested in the safety of his guests he should arrange to speak with me. I was curt and rude. I hung up and called Touse.

Touse balled himself into the chair like a kitten, his eyelids dripping wearily. "I think I will miss you when this is all over," he said. "I'm becoming accustomed to have you call in the middle of the night." He made an effort to smile, but it failed.

"I'm glad you came over."

"Happy to be of service."

"This is probably silly on my part. The bastard wouldn't try again the same night."

"It might have been a mistake, as the manager suggested."

"Do you think it was a mistake?"

"No."

"I don't either." I paused. "Doesn't this remove suspicion from me?"

"Not really. After all, you might be lying."

"I suppose Kelly would have to think that way."

"He's trained to think that way. The probability is that he would think you are more of a suspect than ever. Why else would you manufacture an intruder unless you were guilty of Mrs. Stimmes' murder?" He succeeded in smiling.

"I wish I were lying."

He uncurled. He thought I was lying, I decided. Not until this time did I have the certain feeling that he didn't believe me. Now it wasn't hard to think that Kelly would have the same conviction.

"You son of a bitch! You think I did it. What did I say that gave you that idea?"

He cleared his throat. "You surprise me." He waited as though he expected me to comment.

"For God's sake, I really didn't do it," I said.

"I always had a belief that you might have done it. Had you sat back and let me handle the problems, I would have tried harder to be convinced of your innocence. I began to try less when you began to organize a logical track to other parties."

"The old men? Pratt suggested I wouldn't be seeing him again. That sounded like a threat to me."

"Did it really? The old men are hardly logical as suspects. The prowler was too much."

"Why the hell didn't you say something earlier? I thought you were accepting what I said. What about Seed's visit?"

He didn't answer my question. "Kelly called me when I went back to my hotel. Mr. Lawrence Seed died in his sleep late this afternoon. He has not been out of sight of his sons all day. He fell asleep in his wheelchair, as he apparently was prone to do, and never awakened."

"Nuts! He was here. That blond kid brought him."

"Mr. Seed was being cared for by a nurse."

"You believe that?"

"I'm afraid I do."

"Unless I saw him, how would I know he was in a wheelchair? I can describe him to you. I can tell you what he smelled like."

"These things can be known without meeting him."

"You really believe that!" I screamed at him. It didn't seem possible that Morgan's trap had this tight a lid.

"I'm trying not to believe that."

"Try harder. Everything I've said is the truth. I don't know if the guy who tried to bust in here earlier was a petty prowler or a murderer. I can tell you I feel damn lucky to be alive now."

"And that's the way we will have to leave it." The little-boy's voice was determined.

"Seed dying made the final switch for you. Up to that you were pretty much in agreement or at least coming around to my way of thinking."

"I would rather not talk about it."

"Aren't you afraid I'll kill you, too?!" My whole body ached. I rose from my knot of a position at the edge of the bed. "What do you suggest I do?"

"I'll have to appraise the situation first. Perhaps I've been too hasty in my judgment."

An obscenity almost escaped from my mouth. I could not sit back and wait for the trap to become inescapable. I certainly couldn't wait for a squeaky-voiced lawyer from Washington to make a judgment about my life. It didn't make sense. I was desperate. "I don't care what you believe," I said, standing over him, shaking my finger. "Thinking the way you do, I don't know why you came over here. If I'm going to get killed, I might as well have it happen before someone is stupid enough to accuse me of killing Elizabeth. And I don't need you around. You might stop whoever it is. Then we'd both be disappointed."

"You're being childish."

"You're damn right. I'm being childish."

He rose with dignity, pushed aside my finger, and began walking across the room to the door.

"I need some air in here to get the smell out," I said in admittedly childish triumph. I limped to the window, and yanked down the cord of the venetian blind, clattering the slats into a sudden bunch at the top of the window.

Touse studied me briefly, shook his head, and left.

At that moment I was glad he had gone. At the same time I felt lonely—a strange sort of loneliness. I had cast myself adrift. For whatever Morgan had planned, I faced it now without companions, without help, without Touse. If I was happy to be rid of Touse, I was not absolutely certain that I was up to the task of going my own way.

I turned toward the window.

It sounded like a backfire in the street. Simultaneously the window blew apart and I was covered with glass. I fell to the floor. If I had anywhere inside of me a desire to say "I told you so," I had no one to say it to. Badly frightened, I crept over the broken glass, feeling each splinter rake my knees. I had glass in my face; I could feel the points embedded.

"Damn you, Touse," I said aloud, "why weren't you here?" The sound of my voice was eerie. It was tinged with both fear and anger.

I waited. Nothing more happened. I flipped over to my back. I wanted to know where the bullet went. If I could find its mark on the ceiling, I could be sure that the gun had been fired from below. I might therefore be safe if I stood up, since I was now far from the window.

I had never before realized how discolored the ceiling was. Dark shadows blotched the area farthest from the lamp. There was no sign of a bullet having dug into it. Whoever took a shot at me was located on my level or higher.

I wiggled along to the bathroom door. It was closed. Tentatively I raised a hand to the handle. I expected my hand to be hit. Nothing happened. I turned the knob and pulled the door out. I rose swiftly and jumped inside. I was grateful that hotel bathrooms are windowless.

I dug out the pieces of glass I could see sticking out from my skin. A few small trickles of blood made my face look like something called "The Aftermath." After rinsing my face with cold water, I sat down on the toilet seat. There wasn't a hell of a lot I could do but sit there. I had no desire to be a target again.

"There's more violence to life than I ever suspected," I said out loud. "And it's closing in." My voice had returned to normal.

Nineteen

TOUSE AND I SAT IN THE BACK OF THE CHAPEL. IT WAS a surprising turn-out. I had expected just a handful of people to come to Morgan's ceremony, but I had stopped counting after thirty. I hardly knew any of them. Viola Grafton and Martha Kempton, both looking pale and poor, moved sternly up the aisle to the front row. I was surprised to see Touse's detective Nick there. He ignored my nod.

"Nick's here," I told Touse.

"I saw him," he answered. "I suppose he received an invitation."

A boy in his late teens, clinging to the arm of a handsome gray-haired matron, shuffled stiffly down the stone floor. There was something of Stimmes about him besides his blond-white hair.

"That must be the son," I whispered to Touse. He nodded.

Lester Price came in, glancing about, smiling briefly at several people on the other side of us. Then he saw me and pushed into the aisle. I remembered guiltily that I still had his wallet.

"Big show, huh?" he said too loudly.

He sat down next to me. I dug into my coat pocket and brought out his wallet. "Thought you might like this."

"Christ! Where did you get it?"

Several people looked back at us disapprovingly.

"I'll tell you later."

He opened it and began counting the money. "Five bucks is missing," he said.

I shrugged, hoping he would soon be quiet.

"Is that your fee?" he asked.

I ignored his question.

Kelly came in. He grinned broadly when his eyes fell on Touse. He winked at me. We had seen him only an hour earlier.

"What happened to your face?" Price asked me.

"Cut myself shaving." I had told Touse and Kelly about the shot, but they had seemed unimpressed.

"Like hell," Price said.

I stared forward, hoping to end the conversation.

"Who's that guy?" Price asked.

"What guy?"

"The guy who winked at you."

"A detective."

"Christ, that's right. Morgan's wife was killed. I heard that. They know who did it?"

"No."

Touse was smiling at my discomfort. I leaned toward him. "I don't see any point in being here," I whispered.

"As long as we're waiting, there isn't any point in being somewhere else. We might learn something here."

Price's eyes widened at the sound of Touse's voice. After I settled back, he said into my ear, "Is he kidding?"

"Kidding about what?" I said.

"Does he always talk like that?"

"He always talks like that."

I wondered how many of those present belonged to a branch of the Stimmes family. Some were obviously related, having some facial feature reminiscent of Morgan's.

There was a chill in the chapel, a sort of pervading nipping at the surface of the skin that comes from being surrounded by cold and gray stone. It was a good chapel for last rites. It exuded finality. Despite all the living, I felt the presence of death. There was no need to have a body.

The boy that I thought was probably Morgan's illegitimate son suddenly sobbed aloud and buried his face in his mother's shoulder. She pushed his face away. The boy studied her plaintively. Streams of tears coursed down his cheeks. He didn't make another sound, slowly turning his head to the front. His shoulders, formerly firm, now sagged; his head was slightly bowed. His mother never looked at him.

A bell sounded—a tinkle of a chime. In that audience of quiet, it was compelling. Dipped faces bobbed up expectantly. A scattering of people crossed themselves.

A gray-faced thin man walked in front of the audience. Dressed in a black robe edged at the neck with purple, he rheumatically paced out his steps. Holding a slender fire-tipped rod, he lit a series of candles on the right and on the left. A young boy emerged from the doorway on the side and took the rod from him and disappeared.

"Death is eternal," the gray-faced man said aloud when he faced us. He cleared his throat, stared out over our heads. "Man that is born of a woman is of few days, and full of trouble." He coughed. Without emphasis he continued: "He comes forth like a flower, and withers . . ."

He had a colorless voice. It issued words as if they were meaningless combinations of sounds. The sad poetry from Job fell out without emotion. The drone and the interrupting hacking coughts made Morgan's death ceremony seem a series of punctuational marks without any substance in between.

"But man dies, and is laid low; man breathes his last, and where is he?"

Gaggle, cough, cough.

The heads all around me were dipped, probably more in boredom than piety. Some eyes were closed. Some were thick-lidded with weariness. It seemed odd that Morgan would have chosen a bore to make a comment on his rather unboring life. Perhaps he was at heart a conventional man who believed in the dullness of religious ceremonies. More likely, we were the victims of another Morgan joke. He may have thought it funny to have his mourners fight sleep in order to be dutifully awake.

"Morgan Harper Stimmes was not unknown to me as a person," the Reverend said as he abruptly launched into the eulogy. "I knew him and found him to be the most untroubled of those who sought my advice." Hack, hack. "He told me once that he wanted me to say just a few words about him after he died. He also said that he would not abide my saying he was a good man, for he said that I knew better. He asked me if I thought he was a man who was bad, a man who had evil in him. I told him that I thought not. And he told me that I lied, that all men on earth are evil, that that was the way of the world. I told him that the way of the world was goodness." He was no longer staring over our heads. His eyes seemed to be searching among his listeners. I realized that Morgan had touched this man deeply. Somewhere in their conversations, Morgan had reached into this man's confusions and contradictions and had made it possible for him to speak with some truth. This was not a eulogy, I decided.

He had a spasm of coughing. He wiped his mouth daintily with thin fingers. "You all knew Morgan Harper

Stimmes. Perhaps you knew him better than I. Perhaps not. You all, as I did, knew his extraordinary capacity to consume life. He devoured his own, much like a flame—very bright and very hot. And I think he tried to extend this heat to other lives. I cannot judge Morgan Harper Stimmes, although I saw him bring this fire close to my life." He halted. I could see that he was questioning the propriety of his remarks. His eyes flitted to the bank of candles on his right for an instant. They scraped the floor and then they rested.

"It is not for me to judge," he continued. He coughed. His voice became loud. "It is not for me to judge. There is a higher power who will judge, who must judge." He cleared his throat. His voice was again dull and uneventful. "He asked me not to say that he was a good man. He also said that I should not spend time disturbing those memories you all have of him. He was born; he lived; and he died. May he rest in peace."

"How very interesting!" Touse said to me after the gray-faced Reverend left.

We stood on the chapel steps. Some people passing by stared at us with vague interest, questioning us with their eyes. Most just ignored us and walked quickly past, hurrying forth along the intestinal tract of the city. Some of the wealthy were among us; chauffeur-driven limousines, a block long, jockeyed to pick up their passengers.

"Hello, Mr. Pratt!" I called out when I saw the first of my old men. He must have been sitting behind me, for I hadn't seen him earlier. He looked startled when he looked up at me from the curb. He turned and began walking along the line of cars, apparently searching for his own, certainly trying to avoid me.

"You know him?" Lester Price was at my side.

"Bixey Pratt," I answered. "He doesn't want to know me."

"Better he doesn't know you than knows you enough to hate you."

Touse nudged me. Pratt had found his car. The chauffeur holding his door was the blond boy who had accompanied Lawrence Seed to my hotel room. "That's him," I said excitedly.

"I thought so," Touse said, and with astonishing rapidity descended the few stairs toward Pratt and the boy. "Get Kelly," he said over his shoulder as he went.

"What's going on?" asked Price. I didn't have time to reply. I saw Kelly leaning nonchalantly against the far side of the chapel. He apparently had been watching Touse. He straightened up and was following Touse with his eyes. His smile was gone.

"Kelly!" I called. "Touse wants you!"

Kelly had already started down the stairs, melting through the crowd. I went after him, without the same success in avoiding people.

By the time I reached them, Pratt was ensconced in a corner of the back seat. Glowering and growling at the scene taking place outside of his automobile, he sank quietly back when he saw me.

I saw Nick again. He had been near Pratt's car. When he saw me approaching, he waved and walked up the street.

"Young man," Touse was saying to the husky blond, "surely you remember Mr. Leeds. He remembers you."

"Mr. Pratt," the young man said, ducking his head down to look into the interior of the car, "you say the word and we'll go."

Kelly grimaced painfully. "Mr. Pratt is a law-abiding citizen. He's not going to interfere with the law." Kelly was obviously not too certain. The young man was positive that Pratt would and could. "Mr. Pratt!"

The old man glared at me. "Answer their questions, damn it!"

The boy followed the line of sight and looked at me. He stood up. "I never saw this gentleman in my life."

"You did not accompany Mr. Lawrence Seed to his hotel room?" Kelly said.

"Why should I do that?"

"We're asking the questions," Kelly snapped.

"Mr. Seed is dead. I didn't go with him anywhere." Then, as an afterthought, "I never worked for Mr. Seed."

"I can check that."

"Check it. Go ahead and check it."

Kelly put his head in the car. "Mr. Pratt, I may want to question your chauffeur later. I wouldn't want to inconvenience you."

"No inconvenience. May we go now?"

The chauffeur flashed a grin of victory, slammed the door shut, and circled the car. Just before he lowered his head into the car, he looked into my eyes, his mouth forming a silent obscenity directed at me. Then he was gone. He careened out into traffic.

"The Lord preserve me," Kelly said, staring after them, "I thought I saw the bowels of Hell when I looked into Mr. Pratt's eyes. I saw myself burning." He wasn't smiling. He noticed my reaction. Putting an arm around my shoulder, he said, "It's not much of a living, but it's all I got. That doesn't mean I don't do what I know is right. That's a powerful man, Mr. Leeds."

We walked back toward the chapel slowly. Out of the group suddenly emerged Viola Grafton. She studied the three of us as we approached. Her squat figure halted and she stood with her arms akimbo. Her clothes hung on her like a draped gray-black curtain. She turned her head and looked back. I saw Martha Kempton, who was nodding vigorously.

Viola nodded too and stepped toward us. "Mr. Leeds?"

I hurried toward her.

"I wasn't entirely truthful the other evening," she said. "I have something for you. It's not the tape, but I made a copy of the words. I don't have it with me. Martha and I were talking about what the Reverend said, and we agreed that we were free to help you. I'll take it to wherever you want."

"If you don't mind, I'll send you home in a squad car and pick it up for Mr. Leeds." Kelly had heard the conversation.

"We'll walk, thank you. If Mr. Leeds agrees, I'll give it to a policeman."

"That's fine with me."

"In about an hour," she said. She walked away from us.

"You must have made an impression," Touse commented.

"I think the non-eulogy helped," I said.

We went back to Kelly's office, where I had spent part of the morning before the service. (One item at the morning session amused me and at the same time struck terror to the roots of my being. Kelly had said, "So, someone took a shot at you!" Then he had stared at Touse. "If I were a smart lawyer, I might have tried something like that to divert suspicion." Touse had opened his mouth as if to protest, but he had stopped. He had suffered instead.)

The office, if it could be called that, was a space surrounded by temporary partitions. The chairs were simple and hard. There was that smell that comes with the first few days when steam heat is first turned on.

"Good turn-out," Kelly noted.

"Hmm," said Touse.

Waiting was hard.

Twenty

IT WAS TEDIOUS, BUT IT WAS RELATIVELY SIMPLE ONCE you had the words that were used. Viola Grafton's typescript gave us the words. A police technician ran the tape we had with Elizabeth's voice over and over again, and following the script, took word after word off, sometimes even being able to lift an entire expression. He timed the final product. Then he reproduced it on another tape and removed the awkward spaces of silence between the words.

"There!" he said and played it back for us.

I cannot stand that my father was dishonored while you continued to live with splendid and protected reputations. You will no longer be protected. Immediately after the service of my husband, I will mail to the legal authorities copies and a description of how the originals might be obtained of my father's papers implicating you in the swindle of the Vanishing Indian. If I do not live, someone will mail them. Believe me, you cannot escape. My father kept very good records. You have lived too long in honor.

It was especially chilling because of the very dry unemotional delivery. Elizabeth sounded as if she meant business.

"Can I have a copy?" I asked. The phrase "immediately after the service" struck me as a lever I could use on Pratt.

Kelly grinned. "Sorry, I want to keep you alive until you stand trial for a murder."

I rose "Not funny."

"It wasn't meant to be."

I went back to my hotel room, wondering if I dared to follow my inclination and pressure Bixey Pratt now that I knew what the tape said. The hesitance disappeared when I opened my door. There was a note stuck under it: "I want to see you. Pratt."

He was waiting for me. The little man with the halo of white hair tensely clenched the arms of his chair. In a corner of the office his chauffeur sat sprawl-legged, tugging on the lobe of his right ear.

"Hi!" the boy greeted me.

"I've done you an injustice," Pratt said.

"How so?"

"I didn't think you'd survive this long. People like you usually don't."

I sat in the same hard chair as I had before. "I'll take that as an admission."

"Never take anything as an admission," he said.

"Someone took a shot at me last night," I said. I looked at the young man.

"Don't look at me, buddy. I don't shoot people." He had pulled his legs up and stiffened.

"What was that all about this morning? What is it you want?" Pratt asked.

I ignored his questions. "The police have the tape, the second tape you received. Shall I quote?"

He grunted and waved a hand at me.

" 'Immediately after the service of my husband, I will mail . . .' " I paused. His eyes were on his desk. "Is that enough?"

"Enough." His eyes met mine again. "You mailed the material for Mrs. Stimmes?"

"I don't think that's important."

He seemed to relax. A thin smile crossed his lips. "Then why are you here if you're not here to bargain?"

"You asked me to come. I was curious to find out how important it was to you if I sent Mrs. Stimmes' material."

"Ah! Finally!" He grinned knowingly. "See, George," he said to his chauffeur. "How much is it worth to me?"

"I didn't say that."

"Then what did you say if it wasn't that?" He was angry at my denial.

"I want to know if it's important enough to have me killed, important enough to have killed Mrs. Stimmes!"

"You're upset." He was strangely and suddenly calm.

"Upset!" I stood up. "Someone tried to kill me and you think I'm just upset. I listened to that old man your friend over there brought to my hotel room and heard a lecture about the battle between age and youth!"

Pratt looked perplexed.

"Mr. Seed," the young man explained.

"When the hell did you do that?"

"The other afternoon. He called me like always."

Pratt had the smirk of a very superior person. His reaction made me feel uneasy. "There! I suppose that was the difficulty at the church. Easily solved. I have allowed George to do little things for Seedy ever since his sons began cutting him off. Satisfied?"

"No," I said and rose. I knew that he wasn't either. As casual, as pleased, as comfortable, as secure as he was now trying to look, his hands had returned to the arms of his chair. They were bloodless in their bony hard grip. He was holding on as if he were hanging from a crumbling cliff.

"Wait a minute," he said as I turned to go.

I turned back.

"You're going to mail the package?"

"You bet!" I wished I had a package to mail.

The chauffeur stood up, his eyes coldly appraising me. "You say the word, Mr. Pratt."

"Go ahead, Mr. Pratt. Say the word," I said.

"Bastard!" he spit. His pebble eyes glowed. "You're a dead man!"

I left.

I believed him. My time was running out. Morgan had constructed this puzzle. I had to solve it fast. There had to be a link somewhere between Pratt and the murderer. If there was a link, it had been fashioned by Morgan.

The name of the detective and his agency was still in my mind. It had stayed there. Someone had hired John Sayles to follow me. If Morgan was responsible, why were two detectives involved? Was Sayles my link? I hoped he had been released from the Connecticut jail.

I was impressed by Sayles' office. It was not, as I expected of a detective's headquarters, a run-down rack-and-ruin. It might have been a branch office of a sales company or that of a city doctor. There was a girl at a desk in the waiting room. She was clean and alert. The office struck me the same way.

"I'm sorry, but Mr. Sayles is still out to lunch. Was he expecting you?" she asked.

"I'm afraid not. Do you expect him back soon?"

"He should be along."

"I'll wait."

On the table next to the couch there was a collection of magazines. As I sat down, I picked up one and began leafing the pages. My anxiety prevented any concentration I might normally give the printed page.

"Who shall I say is waiting?" she said, looking up from her typewriter.

"Leeds, Ken Leeds," I answered.

She resumed typing. Then stopping, she looked at me. "Mr. Leeds?"

"That's right."

"Oh."

About ten minutes later Sayles came in. He recognized me instantly.

"Sayles," I said, rising.

"Let me ask you a question," he said without formality. "Were you sober enough to recognize me in the cab?"

"No," I answered truthfully.

"You wouldn't provide testimony against me?"

"I couldn't." I knew we had just made an agreement.

He smiled. "Good. Now what can I do for you?"

"Who hired you to follow me?"

"I've already told that lawyer of yours."

"He didn't tell me."

"A big guy named Morgan Harper Stimmes." He took a long cigar from his pocket and bit off the end, spitting it on the floor. The girl looked pained. "That won't help you, will it?"

"He's dead."

"Yeah, he's dead." He lit his cigar.

"Why did you continue working for him after you found out he was dead?"

"I didn't begin the job until after he was dead."

"Why? Nobody would have known."

"I was paid in advance." His eyes never left me. "You kill the dame?"

"No."

"According to a friend of mine who was listening in on the bug, it sounded like it. Sorry, but he told the cops. He had to. They found the bug, so he tells them what he hears."

"What did he hear?"

"He hears the dame yelling at you. The phone was ringing. She answers it finally, listens, and says, 'All right.' Then silence. Then she was saying, 'Oh no!' She falls. Then my friend gets on the telephone and tries to see if he can reach someone in the apartment. Nobody answers. You were the only one he heard before."

"Dear God," I said.

"The cops didn't tell you?"

"No."

"I would have heard it myself but I was in a Connecticut pokey."

I was stunned. My face must have blanched. He asked me if I felt all right. There were still questions that needed answers. I slowly faced him again. He had a kind of bemused smile as he studied me.

"Whom did you send your reports to?" I asked.

"What do you mean?"

"Listen," I said, losing control, "I'm moving closer and closer to the electric chair! You didn't do all that work, keeping track of me and Mrs. Stimmes, because of duty! You sent your reports to someone, some place!"

Sayles glanced at his secretary. "A blond kid used to come and pick them up. Stimmes told me somebody would come and ask for them. This kid came."

"The blond kid. That had to be Pratt's chauffeur," I said. "How complete were your reports?"

"You sure you're all right? You look like hell."

"I'm fine. How complete?"

"Mabel, give him a copy." He smiled, clamped the cigar in his teeth, and walked toward his office. "Good luck," he said.

Mabel took a carbon from her file cabinet and handed it to me. I read it there in the office. It was complete.

I remembered wondering why Stimmes had chosen a lawyer in Washington. Why had he picked Touse? Now I knew why.

I tried to hail a cab to take me to the police station, but I wasn't having much luck. I saw him across the street, looking at me.

There was a drugstore on the corner, and I dodged into it. It was a busy street and a busy drugstore. I thought I'd be safe.

"Where are you?" Kelly asked.

"I'm in a drugstore."

"Where?"

"What the hell difference does it make? I know who killed Elizabeth."

"So do I. Where are you? I want to know where my prime suspect is." He burbled laughter. "Mr. Pratt has called to say that you broke into his office in a violent mood."

"I didn't break into his office and I wasn't violent. Listen to me! I've talked to the detective, Sayles—Morgan hired him, but he was sending his reports to . . ."

"Come off it! I talked to him, too."

"All right. Whom did he send his reports to?"

Silence. "I guess he didn't," he said finally.

"You guess! He went to a hell of a lot of trouble for a man he knew was dead! He sent them to Pratt." Then I said, "Oh oh."

"What do you mean 'oh oh'?" he asked.

"I mean oh oh." I was looking through the glass of the phone booth and staring at him studying me. "He's outside now."

Something exploded in the front of the drugstore, and people began running around. He didn't. He was walking calmly toward me. There was plenty of dark smoke. The lights blinked off. It was an eerie scene. I watched dispassionately, as if it were personally meaningless.

"Good-bye, Kelly," I said, "the son of a bitch is going to kill me."

Kelly didn't say anything. He had hung up.

I sat quietly. I braced the door closed with my knees. That didn't bother him. He smashed the glass. He wasn't smiling. I didn't know what to say. So I said, "Oh oh."

He held up a long curved piece of glass in his gloved right hand. For an interminable moment it seemed suspended over me. I shrank back and closed my eyes. Then it was over. When I opened my eyes, another man was standing behind him with an arm around his throat. His eyes were bulging. He seemed surprised.

Kelly finally convinced me that I could safely come out of the booth.

"What happened?" I asked.

"You don't think I'd let you go wandering around by yourself, do you?" he answered.

Twenty-One

IT WASN'T THE SAME. IT WAS LATE AFTERNOON. WHERE Elizabeth had sat, Kelly now sprawled. Also, I was different. Before, in Touse's office, I had been on an emotional razor-blade edge. Now I felt tired and had an odd regret that the struggle was all over. The reflex of having a need to react to danger hadn't subsided. There was still a jittery pulsing momentum that hadn't died. I could and would fling myself to the floor at the vaguest signal that there was something threatening. I'd probably close my eyes.

Everyone present seemed exhausted. Touse had a bucket of ice this time—a change—and the whiskey seemed more palatable.

"Do you think Pratt will recover?" I asked. Pratt had had a heart attack in his office after I had left him, and was now in the hospital.

"I don't think I'll ever have to worry about Pratt going on trial even if he lives. Pretty serious coronary. Pretty badly paralyzed." Kelly grinned.

"I'm not going to feel sorry for Pratt," I said. "He was trying to have me killed, too." I held out my glass to Touse. He filled it with whiskey without commenting on my consumption. We were quiet, as though drinking was the only important thing to do.

Finally Touse spoke. "Elizabeth must have been a woman with an enormous sexual appetite."

"Is that meant as a question?" I asked.

"No question. Remember the events prior to your leaving, the night she was murdered? The open door, the telephone ringing. He was in the apartment when you were in the kitchen. He told her to get rid of you and that he would telephone her until you left. At that moment the only motivation she had was sex. And she had no reason to think he would murder her; she had slept with him on a number of occasions. I think she was a woman with brutal passions. She preferred brutality."

Touse was right. I knew that, but there was some pain in knowing that Elizabeth had chosen someone else. The brilliant Touse! Would he also feel some pain if I told him that Stimmes had hired him only because Touse always employed a detective named Nick.

I remembered Sayles' first report to Pratt:

> This Nick Caron is one rough character. I was surprised to see him hanging around Mrs. Stimmes. Thought it was strange. When Stimmes first came to me, he asked if I knew of any detective who worked for a lawyer. I told him that most of us did at one time or another. Then he asked me if I knew of one who did who might be hired to commit murder. I told Stimmes to get the hell out because I wasn't interested in a client who asked questions like that. He said that he was just testing me because he didn't want a detective like that.
>
> After he hired me, I told him about Nick Caron. That's one s.o.b. He would kill his own mother for enough dough, maybe just for a dime. And he's smart. The police like him because he used to be a cop himself.

"I think it's time," Touse finally said. "I have been keeping a letter for you. I was not supposed to give it to you for another week. I've been tempted many times to give it to you. But you know me, Ken. I like to follow the lines of the puzzle and see if I can come up with the solution." He smiled weakly. He took an envelope from the top of his desk and handed it to me.

The front of the envelope had "Leeds" neatly typed in the middle.

"Stimmes?" I asked.

Touse nodded.

I ripped it open and began to read it aloud. There wasn't anything Stimmes could do to me now, I decided.

" 'Leeds, I think that the game is over. I think it must have been a wonderful joke. Though everything I plotted, from the point of planning, was superb, I must have missed somewhere. I really have little animosity toward you and Elizabeth. But for some small time, didn't I chill you both? Didn't you feel that death was close? Let Elizabeth read this note and then both of you can laugh together. There is panic in knowing that you don't fit, and some madness, too. To tell you the truth, I did want to destroy you all. The game was designed initially because of this inner hatred. I almost called it off when it seemed too perfect. Then I remembered. My name is Morgan Harper Stimmes. I'm dealing with modern people who are accustomed to complexity. I wonder. How much would Pratt believe? Would he accept Elizabeth as a person who might blackmail him? It's a pity that I will never know. The game won't work, I decided. Then I saw that it had humor. It was very funny. I laughed and laughed. I hope that you and Elizabeth can now join me in the laughter. Damn it, Leeds, it is funny.' "

That was the end of the letter. I looked at Touse. "You should have given me the envelope before." He didn't answer. He was pale. Kelly rose and, without speaking, left.

I know I still think of Morgan Harper Stimmes during the holiday season when I hear the tinkle of glasses. Even with all that has happened, I don't believe that even I would be very startled if I were to look up at the next party I attend and see the towering blond-haired Stimmes weaving his way through the crowd, laying a hand on the shoulder of a stranger and ducking to whisper some inanity which even a stranger might enjoy, slipping by (satisfied and smug to have caused a smile) to a pretty woman to plant a kiss on her cheek and a compliment in her ear and finally to come to me and greet me, as always, "Leeds, I suspect—just suspect, mind you—that everything is better than it was when it was just wonderful." Then he'd tip his head back and howl with delight at his own fine optimism.

As I said, I wouldn't be very startled. But I would be suspicious about his motives.

I now have a terrible dream to contend with and a new thought about mankind. Being aware of the fact that a dinosaur can exist among us, I've begun looking around me.

I'm beginning to wonder if there are any people.